this is

# ME,

## baby

*Elijah,*

*Sometimes second*
*chances come at a*
*hefty price...*

*♡ K*

# K WEBSTER

Books by Author K Webster

THE BREAKING THE RULES SERIES:
*Broken (Book 1)*
*Wrong (Book 2)*
*Scarred (Book 3)*
*Mistake (Book 4)*
*Crushed (Book 5 – a novella)*

THE VEGAS ACES SERIES:
*Rock Country (Book 1)*
*Rock Heart (Book 2)*
*Rock Bottom (Book 3)*

THE BECOMING HER SERIES:
*Becoming Lady Thomas (Book 1)*
*Becoming Countess Dumont (Book 2)*
*Becoming Mrs. Benedict (Book 3)*

*Alpha & Omega*
*Omega & Love*

WAR & PEACE SERIES
*This is War, Baby*
*This is Love, Baby*
*This Isn't Over, Baby*
*This Isn't You, Baby*
*This is Me, Baby*

To the other half of my heart,

This is ME, baby…and you love ME anyway.

Thank YOU for that.

YOURS

# War and Peace Series Reading Order

"These violent delights have violent ends."
—William Shakespeare, *Romeo and Juliet*

Warning:

*This is Me, Baby* is a dark romance. Strong sexual themes and violence, which could trigger emotional distress, are found in this story. If you are sensitive to dark themes, then this story is not for you. *This is Me, Baby* is the fifth book in the series. Please read the first four books before reading this one to understand the story.

# PART ONE:

"Love Is Not Enough"
by Nine Inch Nails

# PROLOGUE
## Brie

*The day before...*

"I FEEL LIKE FOR ONCE, I HAVE A FUTURE. SOMETHING I can actually look forward to," I murmur and absently rub my still flat tummy. One day it will swell with our baby. The idea both elates and terrifies me.

Duvan chuckles and sits up on his elbow on the bed beside me. In the morning light, his eyes are a brilliant purple, not a trace of black in them. I could stare into them for hours. "I want you to wake up every single day and look forward to the next. You've had too much heartache in your life, mi amor. It's time to live. It's time to love. It's time to be happy. You deserve it."

His fingertip brushes against my bottom lip before he drags it along my throat toward my collarbone. When he skates it over to my nipple, I let out a gasp.

"I'm most definitely happy right now," I tell him with a grin. My nipple stands at attention as if to affirm my statement.

"Good," he growls as he climbs over my naked body. "I won't ask you for much, but your happiness is something I need, tigress. I want it. I desire it. I fucking crave it. Seeing your genuine smile or hearing your sweet laugh is better than any drug I've ever experienced. You're the real deal." His lips dance across mine. "You're mine."

I hook my legs around his hips and slightly lift up from the bed in a needy way. When he's inside of me, owning me and pleasing me, I feel whole. Perfect. A part of something much bigger than I ever dreamed of.

"I need you," I tell him, my voice almost a whine.

He nuzzles his nose against mine before pulling slightly away to look down at me. A strand of black hair falls down over his right eye, and he rewards me with a crooked grin. It sets my skin on fire with the need to have him before I go crazy. "You don't need me," he murmurs. But as he slides his thick cock against my clit, I know it's a lie. I need him with my entire being.

"I can't seem to function without you," I admit. With each slide against me, he makes me wetter and wetter. One wrong move and his teasing charade will be over. He'll be seated deep within me where he belongs.

His thumb strokes my cheek. "You are your own person, Brie. You may need my cock inside of you right now but you don't need *me* to exist. You're like some beautiful planet that hasn't been discovered by anyone but me yet. I come visit because I love being there with you. But you don't need me there to thrive. You exist in the vast black nothingness because you were meant to. You were always the plan…everyone around you, including me, is simply a part of the plan."

Tears well in my eyes and I blame my stupid emotions.

He hardly ever calls me by my name. It startles me to the point that I begin to examine his vague words. I don't like the ominous nature of them. Like he's unknowingly warning me of a life without him.

I can't exist in a life like that.

"Tigress…" His growl has me locking eyes with him. "I'm not trying to make you sad. In fact, in about thirty seconds, I'm going to make you really fucking happy." He closes his eyes for a brief moment before blinking them back open. "I just want you to know that you're stronger than you give yourself credit for. I learned this about you the very first time I saw you. Your face was so impassive yet a storm brewed in your eyes. I could feel the heat of your fury at being a pawn between my father and Heath. That eventually you'd tire of their bullying. That one day you'd incinerate them both with your fiery wrath. I've seen your strength on many occasions. It hasn't been fully unleashed, but baby, it's there."

He swipes away a tear on my cheek and kisses my nose. My chest aches with a dull pain that begins to form there. I hate the tone with which he says his words. As if he and the rest of the universe know something I don't. Something that will completely blindside me one day. Something that will force me to call upon those alleged strengths he's so confident I own.

"Don't ever leave me," I choke out. I'm not sure where the insecurity is coming from but I can't bear the thought of him growing bored with me one day.

His mouth smashes against mine in a deep kiss. A kiss that makes promises he's yet to voice. That he'll be with me forever. I moan into his mouth as he slowly pushes his cock into me. With Duvan, I want him to split me in two. For him to burrow his way so deep into my soul, I'll never get him out.

"I'll always be with you, mi amor," he vows between our wet, breathy kisses. His hips buck in a slow and torturous way against me.

"Here." He taps my temple.

"Here." He runs his fingers between my breasts, lingering long enough to feel my thundering heartbeat.

"And here." His hand splays across my stomach.

I nod in agreement and dig my heels into his ass to spur him on. I need my tiger to maul me. To destroy my being and mark me as his. "Always with me," I echo, my voice quivering with the anticipation of a very close orgasm.

His kiss deepens as he thrusts harder into me. Duvan touches me in all the right places. Says all the right things. Smells exactly the right way.

"Oh, God," I whimper a second before my body convulses with an orgasm.

He grunts against my mouth, his hot breath tickling me, as he finds his own release. His hot semen fills me, but it's actually *him* who fills my heart.

"Tigress," he says, a smug tone in his voice. He pulls away and lifts a black eyebrow at me. The shadow from not shaving in a couple of days is a sexy look on him. My pussy throbs just looking at my handsome husband. "I'm going to make you love me one day."

All I can do is beam at him.

He won't have to make me.

Because I already do.

*I love you, Duvan Rojas.*

# I | Gabe

*The day of…*

LOVE IS STRANGE. AT LEAST THAT'S WHAT I ALWAYS TOLD my baby girl. That it's messy and confusing. That half the time it doesn't make sense. That sometimes, it morphs and changes into something new.

What I didn't tell her is that love is ugly too.

As a father, I wanted to shelter her from heartache and pain. There was no way I was going to crush her and tell her that sometimes love really fucking hurts.

And yet…

I should have warned her. I should have explained to her that sometimes love is like a dull knife that takes pride in gouging out little pieces of your heart, one painful dig at a time.

Love has fucking destroyed my daughter.

Glancing over at the passenger side of the rental car, I let out a sigh of frustration. She looks so tiny curled up in her seat. Her hair is messy and caked in blood. Those high cheekbones, which are exactly the same design as her mother's, are tearstained and almost as red as the blood that covers her.

I tear my gaze from her sleeping form and focus on the dark road ahead of me. The rain is coming down in buckets due to the tropical storm, which makes trying to drive in it a bitch. I'm dying to get on my phone and call War. To flip the fuck out on him for not warning me sooner about what was going on.

*"We can't be sure,"* he'd said. *"Everything looks okay from afar."*

But it wasn't fucking okay. Some motherfucker had a hard-on for my daughter. The prick was supposed to take care of her so she'd be safe and loved. A stand-in father, if you will. This life was supposed to be preferable over the one I could have given her with Hannah. She was supposed to thrive and live life to the fullest.

Not this.

She wasn't meant to be forced to marry some pussy at eighteen, carted off to South America, and then have to witness the brutal murder of her *husband*.

Just thinking the goddamned word has me on edge. My knuckles turn white on the steering wheel as I clutch it with fury.

If only I'd not been wrapped up in Hannah, I could have noticed the signs sooner. I should have known better than to leave Ren and War in charge of looking after my daughter. Those two idiots can't identify evil from a mile away, not like I can. Hell, I'm married to it. I recognize the unhinged parts of people. Hone in on them like a fly on shit. If I'd taken one minute out of my goddamned life with my wife and Toto to look beyond the surface of Brie's new life, I'd have seen the signs. Something would have alerted me.

I could have saved her from all of this.

Clenching my jaw, I attempt to calm the fuck down. My daughter needs me to be her strength. I've got a lot of apologizing to do. I need to fix my broken baby girl.

My phone rings in my pocket, jerking me from my inner hatred. I yank it from my pocket and bark out a harsh, "Hello?"

"How is she?" War demands. "Ren told me what he saw during the Skype session—"

"I could have saved her sooner," I snap, interrupting him. "You and your son were supposed to be watching her. How could you not see any of this earlier? The clues were there, were they not?"

The line is quiet for a moment. "Gabe, is Brie safe?"

"Yes. Now answer the fucking question."

He huffs into the line. "Perhaps if you wouldn't have gone all Bonnie and Clyde with my daughter, you would have noticed the signs your own damn self." Even though his words are meant to bite, they don't.

"*Your* daughter needed me," I hiss back.

"*Your* daughter needed you." His retort isn't pissy...it's matter of fact.

"Jesus," I complain. "This is all my fault."

A commotion in the background on his end grows quiet. "Your other daughter needs you too."

I scrub at my cheek in frustration. I'm fucking tired as hell, having been on a non-stop journey all over the god-damned globe ever since I was first made aware of that sick asshole Heath Berkley. I'd made it my mission to slaughter his ass once Ren told me all about the depraved things he'd done to her. Things he'd witnessed, but also the stories that came from her adopted sister too. I'd called with the intent to check on Toto and ended up slamming my phone down after a long, detailed account of exactly what my daughter had been dealing with.

"How's Hannah? Is she being…"

War sighs and it makes my anxiety spike. "She's being nice. For the most part. We haven't had to restrain her or anything. Toto seems happy to see her."

I let out a breath of relief. "She's still not allowed to be alone with her," I remind him.

"Don't worry," he assures me. "Bay hasn't let Toto out of her sight since Han showed up."

Thank fucking God.

"Are you bringing her back to San Diego?" he questions. "Gabriella can always stay with us in case…" he trails off.

"Hannah loses her shit?"

He huffs. "Bay researched medicines that were okay for Han to take while pregnant. I'm going to order them and have them shipped here as quickly as possible. So maybe—"

War.

Always trusts Hannah can get better.

Hannah will *never* get better.

That, I know for a fact.

"Get the shit ordered," I grunt.

"Do you want to talk to her?"

I roll my head on my shoulders in an attempt to loosen my tight muscles. "No."

Silence.

"She's been asking for you," he murmurs.

"Speaking to me will just rile her up. We need her calm. Tell her you couldn't get ahold of me," I instruct.

I've been driving in the dark for hours. Long after the ferry ride that was choppy as fuck due to the storm. I don't know where I'm going but I'm just getting her far the hell away from that blood bath.

My poor Brie baby has seen too much blood in her lifetime. Her mother and now her husband. If I could rewrite history for her, I would.

"When are you coming back for the rest of your family?" he questions.

I glance over at my broken daughter and sigh. "I don't know. I need to assess how she's doing first. As soon as we've landed somewhere, I'll update you."

Before he can get any more words in, I hang up.

Brie sniffles from beside me. Her tired eyes blink open, and then she tells me exactly where she wants to go.

And of course I'll take her there.

Thirty-one hours is a long goddamned drive. We stopped off at some roach-infested hostel before we entered Colombia. I was able to get Brie to take a shower, but she's been in a state of shock. Thankfully, she's slept most of the time.

The GPS signals we're at our location. Fucking finally. I'm not at all comfortable staying here, but we have no choice. We need to rest for a few days before we travel any further. I feel like it's all I've been doing for the past week as I hunted for that prick Heath. Now that he's no longer a threat, I can focus on my daughter.

She sits up in her seat and squints in the darkness. The house is one of the fancier ones we've seen. I like that it sits on the outskirts of town, far away from any hoodlums. I can keep her safe here for now.

As soon as we park, she clambers out of the vehicle and sprints toward the house. But before she makes it very far, she doubles over and vomits into a bush. I grab the bag I'd stuffed my clothes into, as well as another one I'd filled with some stuff she had at the home on the island. I'm not sure if I grabbed everything she needs, but I didn't want any evidence of her left at the murder scene. I hope I took everything and that she won't get tied back to what happened there.

"Brie baby," I say softly. "Don't just charge in there. Let me make sure it's safe."

She pauses as she starts up the porch steps. Her teary eyes find mine and she nods. "He could be here."

The chilly way in which she says those words causes unease to crawl up my spine. I killed the monster in her world. Fucking stabbed every vital organ I could push my knife into. Heath Berkley can't hurt my daughter ever again. She must still be in shock if she doesn't remember that.

I clutch her shoulder before passing her on the porch. Thunder grumbles nearby and I know we've only been given a brief reprieve from the hammering winds and rain. I unsheathe my knife. Soundlessly, I drop our bags to the floor beside the door and twist the knob. It turns without resistance, which makes alarm bells ring inside my head. The door makes a squeak of protest when I push inside.

Darkness.

I can hear the hum of the refrigerator but not much else.

"Stay there," I instruct in a whisper.

On silent feet, I make my way through the darkened living room. Every few minutes, the lightning illuminates the space, showing me my path. I clear the front room and kitchen first. I'm just walking down the nearly pitch black hallway when I hear the familiar click of a gun being chambered.

Fuck.

I slash my knife in the direction of the sound—at least where I think I heard it—but it's wrong. In the next instant, I'm tackled. It catches me by surprise and I crash into a wall, knocking a picture to the floor, causing it to shatter. My attacker attempts to choke me from behind.

But I'm bigger.

With a roar, I flip the little fucker off my back. He hits the wood floors with a loud thump. In the dark, I wave my knife out in front of me in an attempt to slash him wide open. When I hear the ragged breathing nearby, I lunge forward. But he's too quick and he kicks my knife out of my hand. I manage to find the asshole's throat, gripping it in a punishing vise.

Cold metal meets my temple and I freeze.

And then light.

Blinding fucking light.

"Daddy!" Brie cries out from behind me. "Don't hurt her!"

*Her?*

I glare down at a girl not much older than Brie. Her eyes are wild and her nearly black hair is messy. Her hand—which she is holding a gun with, pressed to me—trembles severely.

"Luciana," Brie says with a sob.

The girl beneath me lets out a cry of relief at seeing my

daughter. They must be friends. I snatch the gun from her grip and rise to my feet. She quickly jumps to hers. Her brown eyes are narrowed as she scrutinizes me.

"This is my dad." Brie runs over to the girl and they hug. When they pull apart, Luciana frowns at her.

"Beh?" she seems to say in question and then taps her heart.

Brie lets out a ragged sob and shakes her head. "H-He's g-g-gone."

Luciana starts to cry too, and the two girls lock together in an embrace. Meanwhile, I stand there looking stupid. I don't know what's going on or how to fucking fix it.

"Are you alone?" I demand with a growl.

The girl looks over at me and nods.

"Esteban…" Brie murmurs. "He's not been by?"

Terror flickers in Luciana's eyes. She shakes her head. Why the fuck won't she talk?

"Daddy," my daughter says. "We're safe. He's not here."

Hot anger surges through me. The fact that my daughter has more than one man to fear has my teeth grinding together to the point that I wonder if I'll break them. I want to grab Brie by the shoulders and shake the answers out of her. Problem is, she's so fragile, I'm afraid it would crush her.

We need to get some sleep and gain our bearings.

Then she can explain this entire fucked-up world she's been living in.

"I'll grab our bags and lock up," I say with a huff. "Luciana, can you make sure she eats something?"

Luciana nods and breaks from their hug. When she starts past me, I snag her wrist. "What's the matter? Cat got your tongue? Why won't you talk?"

She lifts her chin bravely and glares at me. Then, she opens her mouth. I gape at the little stump in her mouth. What the fuck?

"Esteban." The name is whispered from Brie behind me.

This motherfucker is right at the top of my shit list. Jerking my head to Brie, I lift a brow in question. "Who's this Esteban character?"

Her eyes well with tears—I'm surprised she still has any left—and she drops her gaze to the floor. "He's nobody." She pushes past me and I hear her footsteps as she runs up the stairs.

Luciana makes a sound of disagreement. I turn to look at her. Her lips are pressed into a firm line.

"Esteban hurt you?" I demand.

She narrows her eyes and nods.

I grit my teeth and look up at the celling for a moment before meeting her gaze again. "And did he hurt my little girl?"

Tears pool in her brown eyes, making them look like melted chocolate. Her bottom lip wobbles as she makes a motion of giving herself a shot into her forearm.

"HE FUCKING DRUGGED HER?" I roar, my chest heaving with fury.

The young woman flinches at my tone and nods wildly.

"Is that all?" I'm seething mad.

She swallows and shakes her head. My fears come to life when she mouths the word: *rape*.

The wall beside me never saw it coming.

I blast my fist through it. One. Two. Three times until the young woman grabs at my elbow. When I finally turn to look back at her, she's blurry. So fucking blurry. I stiffen when she hugs my middle.

A choked sound escapes me.

Luciana pulls away and reaches a small hand up to my face. She swipes away wetness from my cheek before making a motion of holding a phone to her ear. I pull mine from my pocket and hand it to her.

Her dark hair curtains around her face as she taps away with lightning speed. The heat keeps streaming down my cheeks. I can feel it dripping from my jaw.

My Brie.

My poor baby girl.

She hands me back my phone, and I see she's written a message on my notes app.

*Esteban is an evil man. He cut my tongue from my mouth when I was a little girl. He's done terrible things to Brie. He forced heroin on her and raped her. Many times. Is Duvan really dead? Oscar texted me about what they saw.*

I lift my watery gaze to find her staring at me with such hope in her eyes. Hope that it was all a bad dream. Hope that I'll somehow save her from this motherfucking Esteban, too.

Clenching my jaw, I give her a slight shake of my head before storming off to comfort my daughter. Her broken wails behind me seep their way into my soul and crack it wide open.

Esteban is going to fucking die.

The asshole won't die easily.

I'm going to peel his skin from his sorry body and feed it to him until he chokes to death.

And I'm going to make sure he feels every second of excruciating pain.

Nobody touches my daughter.

Fucking nobody.

# II | War

*Several days later...*

"**Y**OUR MOVE, DADDY."

Hannah's blue eyes glitter with clarity. The meds seem to be working. I don't notice the darkness overtaking her when she looks at her mother or when Toto acts out. She seems...normal.

Of course, with Hannah, there is no normal.

She can never be normal.

My daughter will always teeter on a delicate line between here and...*there*.

We absolutely can't have her go *there* again.

Out of all my children, Hannah's always been my most worthy opponent on the chess board. She's calculating and smart as a whip. That's what makes her so dangerous. The girl isn't just rash and impetuous. A lot of the time, she plans out her moves. Always thinking about the end game. She contemplates the other moves. The outcomes. The consequences.

"You're stuck," she tells me smugly as she sits back in her chair, rubbing her swollen belly. In another few months, I'll have a grandson.

I arch an eyebrow at her and am met with a satisfied grin. She's given me that smile ninety-seven times since she's been here. I count them because I need to figure her out. It benefits my family if I can think several moves ahead of our most unpredictable piece. For her safety...and ours.

"I'm not stuck," I say with a grunt. I have three options to take out her queen within just a couple of moves. But something tells me she knows this and is setting me up so she can obliterate me when I go for the most obvious moves.

She starts humming something sweet, but coming from my daughter, it sounds haunted and borderline fucking scary. Her blue eyes darken several shades as she looks past me out the window at the beach, the moonlight casting an eerie glow on her face. Baylee used to get the same look in her eye when she thought about Gabe. There's no doubt in my mind, Hannah is thinking about him too. And whatever it is, I certainly don't want to think about it.

"When did you know you were different, Daddy? When did you realize you were sick?" she asks and reaches for her mug of tea on the end table. She sips it and looks at me over the steam.

I scrub at my face and shrug. "I don't know."

But that's a lie. I remember the exact second I realized something was completely wrong with me. It wasn't long after my high school girlfriend moved on because I was going insane. Dad was at his wits' end with me. I'd become antisocial and refused to leave my room. But that isn't when the realization occurred.

It happened almost like a crack in a glacier.

Small at first.

Then it seemed to run from me. Zigzagging back and forth away from me at light speed.

I'd desperately tried to hold the fissure together. Dug my fingernails into the black ice of my mind. Watched them rip from my fingers as the divide spread open. The crack became a valley, and I fell. So far, I fell. Into the nothingness. Alone.

That day, I attempted to calculate how many seconds I'd known my mother before she passed away. I'd obsessed over those last moments of her life. Grew confused on the calculations because I wasn't exactly sure of the exact moment she'd left this world. I replayed the horrific scene of her blood and brain matter all over my parents' bathroom over and over again. Sometimes the calculation would vary by a few hundred seconds. Other times just a few seconds.

It maddened me.

I needed to know.

I'd had a burning desire to cut open my head and demand the memories to become clearer for me. To pull out the part of me that actually paid attention in that exact moment. It was then that I went into the bathroom and buzzed all of the hair off my head. Each strand fluttered into the bathroom sink until my flesh-covered skull was on display. The answers were all inside. I just needed to cut them out.

I'd held a kitchen knife out before me and glared at it for hours. Actually, it was fourteen hundred and fourteen seconds to be exact. But who's counting?

I imagined seeing the blood run down my forehead. To see it dripping down over my eyelids, blinding me with red. The very idea of the horror show replaying again was enough to make me drop the knife with a clatter. I'd gagged and gagged and gagged until I expelled my lunch into the toilet. Then, I'd become fixated on the hair discarded in the sink.

How many were there?

Hundreds?

Thousands?

I found a pair of tweezers and a Ziplock bag. That afternoon, I stood in front of the sink counting my hairs. Each and every one of them. Dad worked late that night. When he'd come home, I was still counting. He'd taken one look at me and broken down. Sobbed and sobbed in the doorway as he regarded my crazed self.

And I *was* crazed.

It was the beginning of my confusion. My mental hurricane. My self-hate.

I'd cracked. That afternoon, I cracked and it wasn't until I met Baylee that I was able to bridge the divide. She healed me. Not only did she place bandages on the splits in my mind but she also showed me how to bring the two torn parts of me back together. With steady, sure hands, she stitched me until I was no longer ripped in two. One day at a time, she healed me.

"Your move," I tell Hannah as I slide my rook into place.

She groans. "Ugh! Dad! How do you always know what I'm going to do?"

I'm still smirking at her when the front door swings open and Ren stalks in. He slams the door, and I cringe hoping he didn't wake the babies or Bay. Calder is out with friends. Not that the kid ever sleeps, anyway.

Hannah frowns at me. "He's still mad at me?" Her expression is crestfallen.

I close my eyes and expel a deep breath. Being mad is the biggest understatement of the year. Ren hates Hannah for the path of destruction she left in her wake. I know this because he's screamed it at me on more than one occasion since Gabe dropped her off on our doorstep to go find Heath.

"He's not mad," I lie.

She makes a humming sound but then leans forward to focus on her move.

"I'll be right back, Han. I'm going to go talk to your brother." I stand and press a kiss to the top of her head before striding down the hallway after my boy.

I hate that they once had such a close relationship, yet now he won't even speak to her. Not that I can blame him. Hannah's ruined so many lives with her choices. But what Ren and Bay don't get is that Hannah can't help it. She doesn't operate like they do. Her mind doesn't know the lines of right and wrong. Hell, even Gabe has some sense of right and wrong—otherwise he wouldn't be so damn protective over Toto.

But Hannah?

She's like me.

Darker, though. Unpredictable. Certainly not reachable.

Her mind isn't a crevice that can be pushed back together.

No…

Her mind is a black hole.

Empty. Crushing. Never ending madness.

Anything that gets sucked up into her twisted vortex gets decimated. She ruins people. Lives. Hearts.

Which is why I watch her every move. Just like in our chess games. It is absolutely imperative I learn everything I can about her darkness. Because if I understand it, then I can keep her away from it. Keep my once sweet baby girl in the light. Gabe, surprisingly, keeps her fairly level-headed. But he doesn't understand her. He feeds her inner monster when she's ravenous. He protects her from herself. And protects those he loves from her. But he simply doesn't get her. Not like I do.

One day, I'll learn about her black hole.

I will figure out her inner algorithms. Crack the code of her head. Cross all the *T*s and dot all the *I*s. I'll turn her black hole inside out. I'm so sure of it.

By the time I push into Ren's bedroom, he's standing with his back to me, his shoulders tense. When I reach out and pat his back, he flinches. It's then that I see the bandages sticking out of the neck of his shirt.

"Did you add more to it?" I question.

He turns to regard me. My sweet son—always the boy who did what he could to please Bay and I—is gone. After witnessing the bloodshed online recently, he's been a little fucked up. His steely blue eyes are hardened. All the softness of my son is hidden from me. He clenches his jaw and glares. "I got it filled in."

I'm not one hundred percent on board with my oldest son getting a full back tattoo, but it seems to be therapeutic for him. It started not long after Brie officially moved on from him. Every couple of weeks, he'd get more added on. But after the massacre, he's seemed almost obsessed with finishing it.

"Can I see?" I question.

He shakes his head. "Later. Why is she still here?"

Ren. Straight to the point. Just like his mother.

I let out a sigh of frustration. "We're the only ones who can look after her properly until Gabe gets back. It's not safe for her to be alone…" I trail off. We both know why.

His eyes narrow and his nostrils flare. "I want access to my trust fund."

I gape at his sudden change of discussion. "Why?"

"I'm moving the fuck out of here. The dorms are just temporary, and when I'm not there, I have to come back here. And I can't stay here any longer. This isn't home," he seethes. "Not when that monster prances around as if nothing happened." He rips at his hair and lets out a guttural growl. "Everything happened."

My heart races in my chest. *Thump. Thump. Thump.* I try to focus on my boy rather than the urge to count the loud beats. He needs me. He needs my focus.

"I can give you your money," I tell him, my voice hoarse. "But, Ren, I really wish you would reconsider—"

"THERE IS NOTHING TO RECONSIDER!"

His entire body quakes with rage. Both of his hands are fisted. My son is no longer a boy. He stands taller than me. Nineteen looks good on him. The past couple of months, he's spent more time in our home gym than anywhere else, and his muscles have really filled out. He avoids Hannah at all costs. Lives in his headphones with his music blasting continuously to block out his family.

It's cutting my chest wide open.

I want to fix my boy.

But right now, I have to fix my daughter.

Ren is smart. He'll figure it out. The kid just needs his space.

"I'll write you a check in the morning. Whatever you need," I assure him. My tone sounds resigned to the fact that Ren will only heal if he gets away from his sister, who was instrumental in his life being torn apart.

"Thank you," he manages. Barely. He turns and starts yanking clothes from his dresser and shoving them into a bag. I'm leaned against the wall watching him when the door squeaks open. When Hannah's blonde head comes into view, I open my mouth to ask her to leave us be.

But Ren sees her before I get a chance to.

"Get out," he snarls, his muscled arm quivering with rage as he points at the door behind her. "Get the fuck out of my room and out of my goddamned life!"

She tenses at his words and shoots me a sad look. "Ren—"

He stalks over to her with lightning speed. I tense, preparing myself to yank him away if his temper flares any more. His finger points at her chest as he glares down at her. Their bodies are nearly touching. "I hate you, Han. Do you understand that in your fucked-up little head? Hate."

Tears well in her eyes. "You don't mean that."

He scoffs, narrowing his gaze. "Every word. You ruined my life. You ruined Brie's life."

She tenses at the mention of Brie. I know this look too. The look she regards Bay with on occasion. The one she flashes to Toto at times. I'm not at all comfortable with this look. It's one that screams: *I could make you disappear with a snap of my fingers.*

I fucking hate the look.

"Okay, you two," I grumble and grab Ren's elbow. I drag him away from her and stand between them. "Han, go to bed. Ren, pack your stuff. We'll talk about this later when tempers aren't hot."

Tears roll down my daughter's cheeks and she launches herself into my arms for a hug. I know those tears, though.

They aren't real. They aren't genuine. They're the ones she uses to get what she wants. Right now, she wants Ren to forgive her.

Unfortunately, I don't think Ren will ever forgive her.

"We'll talk soon, son," I say to him, giving him a nod of my head.

"Yep," he grunts out before he goes back to packing.

I usher Hannah out of his room and into hers. We don't speak as I give her the pills that seem to be helping. Once she's settled into bed, I kiss her goodnight and shut the door. Now that she's not acting so crazy, I don't have to lock her in the room at night.

But Baylee and I lock ourselves in our room.

With both Mason and Toto.

You can never be too sure with Hannah.

By the time I make it back to my bedroom, Ren's already gone. I hear the thump of his bass as he peels away.

Poor kid.

My bedroom is dark, aside from the glow from the closet. Toto sometimes gets scared, so we leave it on for her. She's passed out in her pack-n-play. Her blonde curls glow in the light from the closet. God, I love that little girl. Next, I peek in on Mason. He's in a basinet beside Baylee. She swaddled him up, and he looks serene sucking on his pacifier. The boy looks just like Ren did at that age. My heart swells at how beautiful our children are.

"Come to bed," Bay murmurs in her thick, sleepy voice.

I peel off my T-shirt and shove down my lounge pants. As I crawl into our bed, I'm assaulted with her scent. It's a permanent happy place in my mind. So feminine and clean and just Baylee.

"What was all the yelling about?" she asks in a whisper.

I haul her to me and press a kiss to her forehead. "Hannah and Ren." Our eyes meet, both of us wearing matching frowns. "He wants access to his trust fund. He's moving out, baby."

A storm brews in her eyes, and she chews on her bottom lip for a moment while she contemplates my words. After a moment, she darts her eyes to mine. "I don't want him to go, but maybe he'll be happier."

I nod and slide my palm to her hip before slipping it under her shirt to stroke the delicate flesh on her back. "He needs his space. It's better to let him have his money than for him to quit college or something."

Her fingers skim over my chest and she sniffles. "Everything is a mess right now, War."

I lean forward and capture her lips. So soft. So fucking supple. "This mess is ours. We're the only ones who can clean it up. This mess is our responsibility." I kiss her deep enough to draw out a needy moan from her. "But we *will* get it cleaned up. Then we can be happy again."

Pushing her onto her back, I lick away her tears as I strip her out of her clothes. We've only been able to go back to having sex in the last couple of weeks. Thankfully, though, we don't have to worry about birth control because she got her tubes tied after Mason.

"War..." My name on her lips is a prayer. She needs me to fix it all for her. Of course I will. I'll always owe her for fixing me.

"Shhh," I murmur against her mouth as I part her legs and settle myself between them. I tug my hardened cock from my boxers and tease her wet opening. Then, with a low growl, I push into my perfect wife.

Once I'm seated deep inside her heat, I lift up to look at her. "I love you, Bay."

Her fingernails dig into me and her heels press into my ass as she urges me to fuck her. I suck on her sweet tongue as I deliver the thrusts she wants. Exactly the way she likes them. Exactly the right pace.

With every pound into her tight body, I feel my own climax taunting me. It's so close, but I don't want to lose control unless she's unraveling with me. Now that we have two small kiddos to deal with, our sexual times have been limited. I want her to orgasm and give me all of her, even if only briefly.

"Come all over my cock, baby," I urge. My fingers slip between us and I massage her swollen clit. Having been married for nearly two decades, I know exactly where to touch her. I know how many seconds it will take her to explode with pleasure the moment I find her sweet spot.

"Oh," she moans in the softest of whispers.

Her body clenches around mine. It drives me mad with need. My nuts tighten for a brief moment before I'm draining my desire into her.

"God," I say with a grunt and nip at her bottom lip. "You make the hottest sounds when I fuck the pleasure out of you."

She lets out a quiet laugh and grins up at me. Her blue eyes sparkle. "War?"

"Yeah, Bay?"

"I *am* happy." She palms my cheek. "Everything is a mess, no doubt about it. But I'm happy. As long as you're here taking care of me and the kids, my life is complete. You're a good man."

I flash her a lopsided grin. My cock, which had been softening, hardens up rather quickly. "I'm about to make you happy again. Then, we're going to shower." I buck into her hard enough to make her yelp. The time for sweetness is over. It's now time to bring out her claws. I fucking love it when she digs them into me. "And after we shower, you'll make me happy too when you let me suck on that sensitive clit of yours. It's been far too long, baby."

My hips buck powerfully into her. The pain of her fingernails has me groaning with pleasure.

"Don't stop," she begs against the shell of my ear.

I'll never stop.

# Brie

I'M BROKEN.

Used up.

Empty.

Fucking lost.

The pillow beneath me is soaked from my tears. Days and days. They all bleed together. I'm lost inside this vortex of pain. Unsure where it all starts and where it ends. One thing's for sure, though.

Duvan's not here with me.

Heath ripped him away from me. He came into my life, one last time, and took what never belonged to him. The ache in my chest intensifies. A pain unlike one I've ever known claws from within me. It's like a caged beast desperate to escape. But God has punished me—again—for some reason. Because, this time, I'm to manage this beast all on my own. This beast of despair devoured the old one within me. Before that, I only thought it was bad after my mother was taken from me. Now, I realize it wasn't a beast at all. Just some sad little animal.

But the feral animal in me now is not small at all. It's devastated and crushed and growing by the second. The animal is also very angry. She has a thirst for blood. The one she wanted to devour is already gone. That only leaves the thirst for one man.

Esteban.

The cravings that used to surge through me were because of what he could give me. The heroin. Heated bliss that stole all the pain away. I know that if I wanted it again, I could figure it out myself this time. I could drive into the city, purchase the product, and get high.

If I wanted to.

If I didn't have Duvan's baby growing inside of me.

But I don't want to.

The craving when I think about Esteban now isn't about the drugs. It's about making him bleed. It's about punishing him because he deserves it after all he's done. It's about vengeance. I want him to be the recipient of the pain I can't dole out to Heath because he's dead.

Esteban will be the one to pay for the sins of Heath.

I want his blood to coat my fingers as I cut his heart from his chest.

Swiping a tear from my cheek, I sit up and look over at Duvan's empty spot. The first night we'd arrived back home, Daddy tried to comfort me. As soon as the bed dipped with his weight, I screamed at him to leave. I was so afraid he'd steal away the lingering scent Duvan left. That he'd take away the memories of my husband.

Plus, I didn't want Daddy's comfort.

My heart still bleeds from when he left me. When he took

off with my mother's murderer. As grateful as I was that he saved me from Heath, I still can't help but be angry with him.

The tears constantly roll down my cheeks. But it isn't sadness that is threatening to eat me alive. It's fury and hate and anger. I've welcomed them wholeheartedly. Those fiery emotions don't hurt. They crave to do the hurting.

I want to make someone pay for all the wrongs that were done to me.

My eyes settle on a frame on Duvan's bedside table. It's a selfie of the two of us. One of those times when we were curled up watching movies together. Back when we were happy—just like he always wished for me to be.

I'll never be happy again.

Not ever.

Bile rises in my throat, and it once again reminds me that I'll be forced to be happy at some point. I scramble out of the bed and make it to the toilet in time to vomit. This little gift from Duvan has made me so sick.

I close my eyes and wallow in the misery of losing him. Had Daddy arrived ten minutes sooner, he could have saved Duvan too. Life is just unfuckingfair.

My hands shake as I clutch the toilet seat. I glance down at my wedding ring. Yesterday, I found the strength to go through the bag my dad had packed for me. Inside, I'd found my laptop, some pictures of Duvan and I, my clothes, a T-shirt of Duvan's, and his wedding ring.

Now that, I will be thankful for.

My father may have abandoned me but he always understood love. And in a tense, hasty moment, he had the foresight to grab something that was important to me. Now, Duvan's giant ring hangs on the chain around my neck, which

Ren gave me. Safe, just above my heart, where he'll always be.

Just the thought of Duvan's body decomposing in the same room as Heath's corpse has me throwing up again. Tears roll out and my throat stings. If I were to call out, Luciana or Daddy would be here in an instant to take care of me.

But I don't want them.

I want to deal with this alone.

It's mine.

The hurt. The pain. The loss. It's all I have left of him.

Finally, I manage to feel okay and stand on shaky legs. The shower is hot and does something to soothe my soul into a numb state. If I think too hard about it all, I feel over-whelmed. The crushing weight of reality is too much. I crave to cut my wrists open and find my husband out there in the afterlife.

But each time those dark thoughts enter my mind, I think about our baby. It's enough to snuff out those dark ideations.

I tie a towel around my still wet body and shakily make my way into my bedroom. I've been going through every nook of the house finding items that remind me of Duvan. Collecting them. Sorting through his paperwork. Looking through old pictures. Anything to feel closer to him.

I wish I had someone I could talk to. Sure, Luciana has tried via text. Daddy has held me through a couple of soul-crushing cries. But it's not enough. Climbing onto the bed, I grab my laptop and open it up. The Skype app tells me that one of my friends is on. When I open it, I'm oddly satis-fied to notice that it's Ren who's on.

Is he waiting for me to log on?

Does he want to talk to me?

I know from overhearing my dad that his family knows

what happened. Ren was a witness to the horror. It makes me wonder if he was secretly happy to watch my husband die. The thought makes me sick and rage has me dialing him.

The program makes a chiming sound as it rings and then Ren's face is on my screen. I didn't think through my actions. I'm now sitting here, gaping at his haggard face like I'm a deer caught in a pair of headlights. His once navy blue eyes are hardened into a darker color. Almost black. The hair on his face has grown into a stubble. Dark circles ring his eyes from what looks like stress or lack of sleep. If I thought he'd be happy for my loss, I was mistaken.

Ren's my friend.

At one time he was my lover.

He doesn't want my pain.

"Brie," he murmurs. "Jesus Christ."

Emotion chokes my throat but I swallow it down and blink away the tears forming in my eyes. He doesn't ask me how I am. He doesn't blurt out how horrific it was watching two men die just a few days ago. He does nothing but stare at me with his jaw clenching and unclenching.

I don't reply to him. My heart aches too fucking badly to find words. Instead, I let out a ragged breath and stare back. Eventually, I grab Duvan's ring hanging from my necklace and grip it in my fist. Hot tears streak down my face, but again, no words come out.

We remain silent for quite sometime. Me crying quietly and him sending me a thousand words with just one simple expression.

The two of us are different.

Two new people.

Two people scarred and ruined by our pasts.

I don't even know who he is anymore.

And I certainly don't know myself.

After what feels like hours, but based on the clock on my screen, has only been a minute or two, I let out a ragged sigh.

"Have you heard from Ozzy?" My question is a tiny whisper—one I barely push out of my throat.

His eyes close and he nods. When they reopen, his gaze pins me. "He left that day. Said he had to go see his dad." His gaze lowers until it's no longer locked with mine. "He said they had to dispose of the bodies."

Guilt surges through me. I left my dead husband's body in that beach rental and hopped in a ride with my dad. We drove thirty-one hours to my home in Colombia without a backward glance.

Had I been a better wife and not so shaken to my core, I'd have begged my father to call the police. For us to give Duvan a proper burial. But I didn't. I wallowed in my despair. Until I snapped out of it today. Until anger took over. Until clarity began to set in.

Unfortunately, it's too late.

"If you speak to him, will you tell him to call me?" I ask. Just the thought of seeing Oscar broken over the loss of his brother has me nearly in tears again.

"I will," he vows, his voice raw. "Promise me you'll call me if things get too rough. I'll be out there in a second. Just say the words, Brie."

I force a smile but I don't think it even reaches my lips. It feels as though my lips simply twitch instead. "I'm fine."

"Brie…" His brows furl together. "Be careful."

The tone of his warning has a chill shivering through me. "Take care of yourself, Ren."

As soon as I end our call, despair crashes back down around me. I clutch Duvan's T-shirt to my heart and curl up on the bed. My stomach growls after having emptied it, but I don't move to get up.

I never want to get up.

One week is all it took to dry up. I went from crying at every turn to walking around like a zombie. Luciana is barely able to get me to eat when she tries. Which is often. My dad tries to get me to speak. But I have nothing to say. I'm a shell. Simply going through the motions.

That is...

Until Ren calls me.

Our Skype conversations aren't really conversations at all.

They're more like staring contests. I listen to him bounce a tennis ball off the wall while Nine Inch Nails blares in the background. He watches me as I thumb through photo albums of when Duvan was a kid. Ren occasionally barks out at Calder. I, at times, yell at my dad to leave me alone. We're both sort of existing on the same plane but never intersecting.

I don't understand what's going on inside his head. But I sense the fury just below the surface. I like that he's angry for me. The heat from his wrath warms me like rays from the sun on a warm California summer day. I'm curious about the anger rolling from him. Ren was always so gentle and sweet. I've never really seen him get mad about anything.

I crave to scratch my fingernails along his flesh until the irritation seeps out. To see exactly why it exists. To prod until it becomes infected and spreads. I want to see more of it.

His anger feeds mine.

My inner animal craves to devour it.

"Where do you want them to put the couches?" I hear Calder question him.

My brows furrow together and I sit up to listen better.

"Don't know. Don't care. You're a big boy," Ren grunts. "Figure it out."

When Calder leaves, Ren goes back to bouncing his ball off the wall.

"Couches?"

His head snaps over to the screen and he frowns. "Moved out."

"Of the dorms?"

"And house," he grumbles.

He's angry and this time it doesn't seem to be about me. I'm dying to know what's upsetting him. I feel like he's holding back from me.

"Why?" I murmur.

He yanks off his baseball cap and tosses it away. His dark brown hair is messy. Longer than I remember. A lock of it falls into his eye for a brief moment before he rakes his fingers through his hair, pushing it back. Dark eyebrows furl together and his blue eyes darken. "Hannah. I can't stay there while…" he trails off. His eyes flicker with rage and it ignites something within me.

He can't stay there because of what she did to my family.

I'm not sure why that makes me happy, but it does.

I feel as though I won some battle I didn't know I was fighting.

"How can you afford it?"

He shrugs. "Dad let me into my trust fund. Calder's rooming with me because he doesn't like our fuckwit sister either. Plus, I don't think he's keen on being the backup babysitter at every turn."

I fight a smile imagining big 'ol Calder with a baby in his lap watching *Terminator* and eating greasy pizza. He'd be a terrible babysitter. Calder would probably give the baby Mountain Dew in its bottle or something.

My hand automatically splays out over my own belly. Would Duvan have been like that? Would he have been a laid back father or would he have been overprotective?

I guess I'll never know.

"You going to stay there forever?" he questions. "I mean, it's your house now, right?"

I swallow before dragging my gaze over to a pile on the bed. I've gone through all of his paperwork. When I'd been here before, Duvan would bring things for me to sign. I didn't pay much attention because I didn't care. Only cared about being with him—not his assets. But now…

I realize I have a lot to deal with.

For one, I have to figure out what to do with this house. I'm not sure I'll stay here but if I don't, I'll need to sell it. And his building where he manufactured his coke, I'll need to figure out what to do with that. If I could get a hold of Ozzy, he could help me. But according to Ren, he's gone AWOL.

So has Vee.

I haven't tried to call her, but Ren said he's called many times and even went by her apartment a few times. She's just gone. I know my best friend. Despite Heath being a lunatic, she loved her father. Watching him die had to have been

31

hard on her. She's probably holed up at her parents' house in mourning.

I miss her.

"Brie…"

I blink away my thoughts and look at Ren. His face is scruffy from not having shaved for several days. That, coupled with the fierce gleam in his eyes, makes him look rougher. So different than the boy I remember.

"I guess one day I'll come back. There's just so much to deal with here first. Have you been able to get ahold of Oscar?"

He shakes his head. "Nope."

I'm about to say something else when my door cracks open. Daddy's watchful eyes find me. I wonder if he ever regrets leaving me. We haven't even spoken about it. Simply gone through the motions.

"I need to go," I tell Ren.

"I guess I need to as well. Calder isn't the brightest crayon in the box. Those couches will probably end up in his room," he complains and stretches his arm forward to end the call. His shirt slides up his arm and reveals some black from a new tattoo hiding beneath.

"New tat?"

"Yeah. It's still in progress."

"Can I see?"

He gives me a half smile that warms me and nods. Then, he grabs the bottom of his black T-shirt, peeling it off his body and up over his head. The first thing I notice on the gritty Skype image is how big he's gotten. When we were lovers for that brief stint, he was built but lean. Now, he's massive. Every surface of his chest is hardened and defined. His tribal wave tattoo has been added to and covers the entire upper half of his chest, whereas before it was small and only covered his pectoral muscle.

But what has me curious are what appears to be black tendrils or something creeping around his rib cage and collar bone. Like some creature is behind him and is about to drag him away. It's spooky but looks good on him.

"It's a back tattoo. I'm still having it worked on," he tells me as he turns.

When his back comes into view, I lean forward to get a better look. Even with the pixilation from our spotty connection, I can tell it's really well done. From the base of his skull to nearly his ass is a giant tree. No leaves. Just gnarly branches and roots that seem to reach around the sides of his body toward the front.

"Wow..."

He lets me stare at it for a few minutes. From behind, he hardly looks like Ren anymore. His shoulders are broader, his neck a little thicker, and his back is rippled with newly defined muscles.

"Do you just work out all the time? To hell with school," I tease. Or at least it's meant to come out in a teasing way. But lately, I'm not me and as soon as the words leave my mouth I realize they seem more condescending and borderline rude.

He turns back around and glares. I'm not used to his hardened gazes. A shiver ripples through me.

"I'm only taking a couple of classes this semester. I needed a break. Both are online courses. So, yeah," he grunts. "I've been using my extra time to lift."

I chew on my bottom lip as I stare at him. "Will you be on later?"

He grabs his T-shirt and starts to put it back on. "I'll find you, Brie." His head pops back through the shirt and his steely blue eyes are on mine. They make promises I don't understand. Promises I don't want to understand. His words, although simple, are thick with double meaning.

"Right," I say with a slight shake of my head. "Talk later."

Quickly, I mash the button to end our call. When I look back up, Daddy is still in the cracked doorway.

"Come in," I groan. I'm not in the mood for him to try and talk to me. I'm not in the mood to eat. I'm not in the mood for anything.

He pushes through the door and strolls in as if this is his house. Walking past the bed, he makes his way over to the window. With his back to me, he speaks in a gruff tone. "Are we going to talk about what happened?"

A shiver trembles through me. "You saw what happened. You were there," I bite out.

He looks at me over his shoulder, his brown eyes narrowed. "Not that, Brie baby. Us. How I left you."

Pain stabs at me from the inside out and I have to break our gaze. I look down at my hands to keep from crying. "I didn't understand why you left me. I still don't understand. It hurt so bad, Daddy."

His footsteps near, but I still don't look back at him. He moves the laptop and then sits beside me. I don't fight him when he takes my hand. Truth be told, I miss my dad's comfort. I miss how close we were. Mom was always working so it was me and him. Always.

"I thought I was doing the right thing. When I left you, I never meant for anything to happen to your mother. And then…" he trails off, his voice hoarse.

"Hannah cut open Mom's throat," I remind him, my tone bitter.

He squeezes my hand. "I didn't know she'd done that. I swear I would never have left you to find such a terrible scene. But then, it wasn't safe to come back home. I was a wanted man. I mean, I've always been a wanted man, but the spotlight was back on me. They'd have taken me to prison the moment I came for you."

The thought of Daddy in prison saddens me. I remember being a little girl and him warning me. How he said that if he ever got taken away, that he'd always loved me. That it was never a lie. Our love was real. I'd never understood it at the time. But after Mom died, his real story was all over the news. The terrible things he'd done in the past. The people he'd killed.

It should have made me afraid of him but it never did. The dad I knew wasn't like that. At least not with me. And when he'd eliminated Heath, all I wished for was that he'd done it sooner.

"Heath Berkley imprisoned me. I was his little pawn," I choke out.

I can sense his rage from beside me. It's like a wave of hate clouding the air around us. It doesn't suffocate and destroy me. Instead, it warms me. I breathe it in and hold on to it.

"War was supposed to make sure you were safe. I swear, baby, I kept tabs on you. A few times, I even snuck into that fucker's parties just to get a glimpse of you. Each time, you looked so…"

He must have seen me hanging out with Oscar and Vee. When I was with them, I was happy.

"Ren looked after me," I tell him and finally meet his gaze.

Daddy's eyes are bloodshot and his brows are furled together. His beard has thickened since we've been here. "He didn't do a very good job," he utters under his breath.

I feel oddly defensive over Ren. Sure, he wasn't protective like Daddy or even Duvan. And when his secret came out, I was crushed. But Ren was always there for me. He loved me when not many people did. He made me laugh. He made me feel. He gave me hope in an otherwise hopeless environment.

"You don't know anything about him," I tell him firmly. "How did you know to come find me, anyway? Why didn't you come sooner?" I want to scream at him and say, "Had you been there five minutes earlier, I would still have my husband." But I don't. I bite back the nasty words.

"Ren," he admits with a huff. "He spilled the beans about Heath and that he'd forced you to marry. That he was involved with the Colombian cartel. That he was a motherfucking dragon, and I'd willing left you there. He told me the ways he would touch you. How he'd hit you. All I saw was red. I'd sat by thinking you were happy. That you would go off to school and get a degree, like your mom. That you'd do great things in your life without my toxic decisions affecting you any longer. But it wasn't that way. You were nothing but a goddamned prisoner primed to marry into another bad family."

I shake my head. "Duvan was a good husband. Don't speak badly of him. And Oscar is my friend. The only bad person in this family is Esteban."

He scratches his beard before pinning me with a heartbroken look. "Luciana told me what that scum did to you." His palm finds my cheek and he strokes it. Fire blazes in his eyes as he spits out the words. "I promise you, Brie baby. I will find him and I will make him pay. It won't be a simple shot to the head either. I will torture him. Drain him of all his blood—one drop at a time. He'll suffer because he made you suffer. He'll hurt because he made you hurt. He'll die and you will live. Even if it's the last thing I do, I'll make sure he dies under my watch."

My heart flutters at his words. Esteban may not have killed my husband, but at one time, he killed my spirit. He'd made me hate myself. I want him dead. "Thank you."

Surprise flickers in his eyes but he schools the look away. "Baby, I need you to know that I'm never leaving you again. I know we'll never have a traditional family—and quite frankly, Hannah is difficult—but I'm going to find a way to make it work. We'll find a way to live together. Toto will love you. She's so beautiful and funny. You'll really like your sister."

An ache presents itself in my chest. I shake my head at him. "I'm not going to live with you. I am eighteen now and a widow. I've been imprisoned for far too long. I won't be locked away again."

Hurt flashes in his eyes. "But how will you live? Where will you live? Here?"

Reaching over to the stack of papers, I hand them to him. "All of this is mine. And this," I point at the address of the manufacturing plant, "is my business. At least my part of it."

His eyes widen. "You can't be serious. You're not going to be some cartel queen, Brie. I won't fucking allow it."

Gritting my teeth, I snatch the papers from him. "You don't have a say in the matter. Besides, I'm not going to run it. I'm going to sell it. That's where I'll need your help. I'm afraid these people are dangerous."

His gaze softens and a smile plays at his lips. "You look just like your momma. Alejandra had the same fire in her eyes when she was passionate about something. Beautiful. You've blossomed into an amazing woman. She would have been so proud of you. I certainly as fuck am. You've been dealt some bullshit and yet here you are. Alive. Fire blazing in your eyes. Fierce." He drags my wrist over to him and his thumb swipes over the heart with Duvan's name in it. "The tiger stripes are fitting. Anyone who fucks with you will meet the claws."

My heart patters and a genuine smile tugs at my lips. It's been so long since I actually laughed or truly grinned. Daddy always had that way of being able to cheer me up no matter what.

"I missed you," I admit, my throat tight with emotion.

He tugs my wrist until I'm flush against him. My dad always smelled so good. Safe and loving. A scent I couldn't seem to recall when I was living with the Berkleys but I missed it so badly. Now, I inhale it and hope to never lose it again.

"Brie baby," he whispers against my hair before kissing my head. "I'm not ever going anywhere again. I'll always be there for you if you need me. All you have to do is say the words. I'll slaughter anyone in my path to make sure I get to you."

I hug his middle. Tears roll out, but this time they are ones of relief. I don't feel so alone with my dad here to help me fight my war. His vow can be felt all the way into my soul. He won't leave me again. We're in this together.

"These Colombians won't know what hit 'em," he says with a chuckle. "Mickey and Sylvia are on the warpath."

I crack a smile. "Nobody puts Baby in the corner."

He pats my back. "Damn straight."

"Daddy," I murmur and look up at him. "I'm pregnant."

His smile falls from his face, and for the first time ever, a look of distress passes over my father's fearsome features.

# IV | Gabe

THE SENSATION OF BEING WATCHED HAS REALLY BEEN fucking with my head. Of course I don't mention it to Brie or Luciana, but someone is out there in those woods. I can feel it with every fiber of my being.

And tonight, I'm going to find out whom.

I located Duvan's weapon stash. Found me a big fucking knife and a Glock. Tonight, after the girls go to bed, I'm going hunting. If it's that Esteban asshole, I'm going to enjoy the hell out of skinning him alive.

"Still no word from Oscar?" Brie's voice carries out into the hallway from her room. She doesn't talk much, but each day is getting better. Ever since we had our heart to heart a few days ago, her spirits have lifted. She's still gutted over the loss of her husband, but I see signs of my child hiding behind the sadness. My baby girl lurks inside, just waiting to come out when it's safe.

I'll make her world safe for her if it's the last thing I do.

I'm sitting in her yellow office with the lights out and my

eyes trained on the tree line past the barn. I know whoever is out there can't see me from this vantage point so it gives me the advantage. Eventually, I'll find this motherfucker.

"Where do you think he is?" she asks, her voice somewhat muffled.

I can't hear what Ren is saying but I know it's him. He's the only person she truly talks to. Sometimes, they do this weird-ass thing where they don't talk at all. As much as I want to ask why they do this, I don't. Whatever sort of comfort he provides her seems to improve her moods. Ren, despite being War's kid, is actually okay in my book. I'd much rather have her talking to the likes of him than that Oscar kid she keeps fretting about. I don't trust these Colombians as far as I can throw them.

I still can't believe she's pregnant. With Duvan's child, she later told me. I'm too young to be a grandfather. Hell, I have a baby of my own on the way. She stunned me speechless. I'm still trying to process her words. Not only do I have to protect my baby...but I also have to protect my baby's baby. I think I'm going to develop a fucking ulcer from all this stress.

Something glows for a brief moment beyond the trees, jerking me away from thoughts of my little girl's stomach swelling with child, and my suspicions are confirmed. Someone is out there. Their cell phone just gave them away.

I slip out of the room and creep down the hall past Brie's room. Luciana has already retired to her room above the garage for the evening, so I'll be able to sneak out undetected. The last thing I need is one of those girls following me out there and getting themselves hurt. I make my way out the front door and then creep around the massive house until

I reach the backyard. Darting through the shadows, I make a wide arc to the woods. I move like the night. The fucker won't see me coming. Once I get into the thick vegetation of the forest, I have to slow down and be mindful of my steps as not to alert the prick to my presence. As I near, I can hear his breathing. He's crunching on some leaves. When his phone lights up again, he lets out a groan of frustration as he quickly answers it.

"Yes," he hisses. "I'm here. Where are you?"

He nods his head as he listens and his eyes remain fixed on the house. I inch forward and draw my knife, ready to exact damage on the lurker.

"She's here. Some man is with her." A pause. "Could be. They don't come out much." A pause. "Haven't seen Esteban." A pause. "Trust me, I will, hermano."

I'm much closer now and can hear the voice speaking rapidly on the other end, although I can't make out the words. The fucker is bigger than me. Broad shoulders. Looks meaner than hell. But I'm the one with the element of surprise here. I'm the one with my weapon drawn and ready.

"You think he'll come for her?" he asks, his voice weary. "Has Camilo even spoken to Esteban since Duvan ran him off?"

I don't make out what the other person says but I'll find out soon enough.

"Right. I'll keep watch. Call me when you need me to do it."

It takes everything in me to wait until he ends his call before I pounce. He's not going to touch one hair on my daughter's head. Grabbing the back of his jacket, I yank him backward and push the knife against his throat. It isn't hard enough to puncture the flesh but if he moves, he might cut himself wide open.

"Who the fuck are you?" I seethe. "And why are you stalking my daughter?"

He raises both hands in surrender. "Chill out, hombre. I'm here to protect her," he says through clenched teeth. "Not hurt her."

"Name," I bark.

"Rafe."

"Do you know my daughter?" I demand.

He groans. "I've met her once but I'm not even sure she remembers me. Although, I'm sure Duvan probably spoke of me to her. I'm his right-hand man. His protection." He lets out a hiss of frustration. "Was. I was those things. Now, I'm hers."

He is nothing to her.

I'm her motherfucking protection detail.

"Who were you talking to?"

"Oscar."

The name has me calming a bit. I draw my gun and step away. "Turn around."

He slowly turns around and regards me with narrowed eyes. "Listen, old man," he grunts, "you're in the lion's den out here. Word has gotten out that Duvan was murdered. I have some trusted men protecting his factory and I'm looking after his wife and the house. But it won't take long for the enemies of the Rojas family to pounce on this weakness. Esteban is missing. Duvan is dead. And that just leaves Camilo and Oscar to pick up the pieces. Camilo is at the shipyard eight hours away, and Oscar is with him until he can come out this way. We need to get the little princess out of here before she's in the middle of a drug war. Diego Gomez is just waiting to make his move and steal the Bogotá territory. It's only a matter of days before he can assemble a big enough army for what will be a hostile takeover."

Once again, I'm furious at myself for having let my daughter go. She was sucked up into something a thousand times more dangerous than Hannah. At least with my wife, when she gets crazy, I can manhandle her and tie her ass up. This whole Colombian army shit is way out of my league.

Fuck!

"Walk," I bark out. "We're going to talk to Brie and Luciana about this. If they even look at you wrong, I'm putting a bullet in your skull and letting the fucking forest animals snack on you. No funny moves. You do not know who the fuck you're messing with."

He sighs and nods. "Oscar told me you eliminated that sick fuck, Heath. There's been a hit out on him for years. Gomez just couldn't ever get to him. The Rojas family never got rid of him because he was an asset. I know Duvan hated him, though. You just carried out your son-in-law's wishes."

I motion with my gun toward the house. He trots through the brush and across the grass. Once we're on the porch, he turns to regard me.

"You may not trust me, but Duvan did. We were thick as thieves. He always took care of my mother and sisters when money was tight. I want to return the favor and make sure his woman isn't harmed. It would appear you and I share the same interests, hermano."

The man smirks and it boils my blood. "I don't fucking share," I growl out before I pistol-whip him upside the head. "And I'm not your brother."

Brie sits perched on the arm of the couch with her dark eyebrows furrowed together. She glares at Rafe tied to a kitchen chair I dragged in here. Blood drips from his brow, where I've hit him. He still hasn't come to. The fierceness rippling from her is so thick in the air, you could cut it.

"Did you have to knock him out, Daddy?" Her brown eyes cut to mine and irritation flickers in them. She may have her mother's features, but the look in her eyes is all mine. I've seen it a thousand times in the mirror.

"I don't trust him," I grumble. Walking over to him, I grab a handful of his black hair and yank his head back. "Wake up, asshole."

His eyes slowly blink open, confusion twisting his features. When his eyes lock onto my daughter's, he smiles. If I didn't think she'd beat my ass, I'd knock him out again. "Hey, Brie. Remember me?"

She stiffens and tears her gaze from his. Her fingers twist together. I can tell he makes her anxious and that makes me really fucking anxious.

"You have exactly three minutes to make that look on her face disappear, punk," I snap. "Get to talking real fast." I release his hair and sit down in the chair beside him, my gun casually pointed at his head.

He side-eyes the gun before looking at her with a less confident expression. "Brie. You may not remember me, but I came here once when you two were first married. Remember, you went and fetched us the blow?"

She squints her eyes at him. "I remember there being several men there but I'm not sure."

He frowns. "Do you remember getting high out of your mind on Ex at the restaurant? I drove you two home that night."

My blood boils that her asshole husband gave her drugs. I'm glad the prick is dead.

"I thought you looked familiar. The name is familiar, though. Duvan did speak highly of you," she murmurs. "My dad says Oscar sent you? Why isn't he answering my calls?"

Rafe lets out a sigh. "Duvan and Heath left a mess for little Ozzy and Camilo. With Esteban hiding who the fuck knows where, they've got their hands full trying to keep control of their operation. Oscar has made it known, though, that I am to protect you and to get you out of Bogotá as soon as possible."

Brie's eyes flit over to mine, questions dancing in her eyes. She's eighteen goddamned years old, for crying out loud. This isn't something a woman her age should be dealing with. I'm keen on the idea of getting her the hell out of this country. I can protect her better on my own soil.

"My dad," she tells him, "and you, for that matter, can keep me safe from Esteban. I'm not leaving until I've settled my husband's assets. I owe it to him." She bites down on her bottom lip and her eyes become watery. "Did Oscar mention anything about Duvan's body? Did they bury him or cremate him?" Her shaking hand finds her necklace and she fingers his ring that sits on it.

He shrugs. "He just said that he had his men take care of things in Venezuela. I didn't ask much else. But, Brie, I was serious. We need to get you out of here. You're a target now that Duvan's gone. Diego wants that factory and—"

Holding her hand up, she nods her head. "Good. Set up a meeting with him."

Both Rafe and I growl at the same time. "What?"

Her eyes dart between us. She straightens her back and presses her lips together in a firm line. Then, she speaks in a calm tone. "If he wants it, I'll sell it to him. All the product, the building, the territory."

"He wants to take it," Rafe snarls. "Not buy it."

She stands and crosses her arms over her chest before leveling him with a glare. "You worked for Duvan, did you not?"

He nods.

"So now you work for *me*. Set it up. He'll buy it or he won't get it all. I'll sell it to Camilo if he's not interested."

Rafe shakes his head in vehemence. "Little girl, you don't understand. That operation *is* Camilo's. Duvan just ran things. You can't fucking sell a territory out from under a cartel king pin. You just don't understand!"

His tone is pissing me right the fuck off. I'm about to shut his ass up when Brie snaps.

"I understand things clearly. That building," she bites out, "legally belongs to my husband. I have the paperwork to prove it. I also have the paperwork he had me sign that puts me as a co-owner. Same goes for his house. His land. His money. It's mine. And, as a result, so is this territory. Duvan and I spent many late nights discussing his business. He always wanted me to rule with him. I wasn't just some trophy wife. Camilo receives a cut. That's it. When I sell it, Camilo will get his cut as pre-negotiated. Now, you can either help me, and honor your friend and employer's wishes or you can disobey a direct order." She stands directly in front of him with her hands on her hips. The anger emanating from her is hot like a flash fire. If he's not careful, he's going to get burned. "I have no qualms about having my father take you out back and punish you for insubordination. Do you remember how Duvan dealt with those who were against him?"

Rafe's shoulders hunch in defeat. "You don't have to kill me, little princess. But just remember this discussion when Diego has his knife at your throat. When he steals everything you once owned. Including your life."

Brie doesn't flinch. I'm about three seconds from disemboweling him in her living room but I hold back, just barely.

"My life was stolen last week when I tried to hold my dying husband's throat closed. It drained away along with his blood. Diego can't take anything from me that hasn't already been taken." She darts her gaze over to the clock. "Set up a meeting for tomorrow. Tell him I'm not here to play games. I'm here to do business."

# V | Brie

OF COURSE THE FIRST TIME I SEE DUVAN'S BUILDING would be after he's dead. He won't be there to show me around. It'll just be the three of us. Me, Daddy, and Rafe. Once we realized Rafe wasn't there to hurt me, we untied him. He's much like Duvan was in the fact that he worries over everything. These guys are full of heart. They may be hardened coke kings but they're soft inside.

Diego actually agreed to meet with me. Rafe suspects a trap. Daddy wants to murder everyone. And I just want to do what Duvan would have wanted. He would have wanted me to sell his assets and get the hell back to California. My safety was always his primary concern.

We pull up to a gigantic metal building, probably forty thousand square feet in size, located on the outskirts of town not far from the house. Several employees' cars are lined up in the grass outside. Rafe assured me business continued on as usual in Duvan's absence despite him being in Venezuela with me. They will have learned of his death by now but won't try anything stupid. The punishment for stealing or trying to con your boss is death. End of story. Most of the people working in the coke warehouse are fathers and mothers. People simply doing their job to provide for their family. At first, I'd wanted to judge them. Being a spoiled girl from the US, I secretly scoffed and thought they were terrible people.

Until I realized it was how Duvan provided for his family. With Duvan, it didn't seem as bad. Just like the many times I'd partaken in his drugs. It simply didn't seem like the dirty drug world I'd learned about. It was different.

"Who's the guy with the assault rifle strapped to his chest?" my dad questions from the back seat.

"There are seven more guys like him surrounding the property. Duvan always had proper security, but after what happened with Esteban, he upped it. They're here for our safety," Rafe assures me before climbing out of the car.

Dad and I follow after him. I'd not bothered to dress fancy for this guy. I'm wearing a black pair of yoga pants and a fitted white tank with a pair of tennis shoes. My hair, which has gotten a little longer, is pulled into a messy bun. I've gone without makeup too. This Diego character will have to get over it.

Rafe speaks in Spanish to the scary looking guy with the big gun. But after a long gaze at my father and I, the man motions for us to go inside. Once in the door, we pass by a room lined with glass windows. Inside, more men with guns stand guard as people undress until they're naked. They hand them uniforms to wear. After they're dressed, they disappear through a door which must lead somewhere else in the factory.

I pick up my pace to keep up with Rafe. He strides along

the hallway at a breakneck speed. Dad takes up the rear. When we come to an office door at the end of the hallway, Rafe uses a key to unlock it. He ushers us inside.

As soon as I enter, my heart drops to the floor. The room smells of Duvan's lingering cologne which causes a pang in my chest. I inhale his familiar scent with deep gulps of air. I'm desperate to lock his scent up inside of me and never exhale.

"Have a seat," Rafe says and motions to Duvan's chair.

I walk over to the expensive leather desk chair and plop down. There aren't any pictures, which I'm sure is for my protection, but when I wiggle his mouse, there is a picture of us saved to his desktop.

It was from one of the times when we first got together and I was high as a kite on blow. His tatted up arm is draped across my tits. I can almost recall exactly how he felt at that moment. Soft yet so strong. In the picture, his lips are to my ears, telling me naughty secrets. My eyes are almost black with dilation and my lips are parted with desire.

"How much time do we have?" I question, swallowing down my emotion.

Rafe flicks his gaze to his watch. "Forty-five minutes or so. Knowing Diego, he'll show up late to make a statement."

I give him a clipped nod. "Can you show my dad the place? I'm going to look through Duvan's computer a bit. I want to make sure I'm ready for Diego."

Rafe lets out an annoyed sigh but nods. "Sure. But here," he says and pulls out a handgun, slapping it on the desk in front of me. "It's loaded and ready to go. Just point and pull the trigger if anyone so much as looks at you wrong."

My eyes dart over to Daddy's. He merely nods in agreement. I'm still staring at the gun long after they've gone. If

Duvan were here, he'd probably take me out back and show me how to shoot it.

Thinking about the *could have beens* is depressing. Focusing on the task at hand, I type in Duvan's password and begin rummaging through his files. I make sure to email myself any and all pictures of the two of us he has saved before I do anything else.

Soon, I become engrossed in his notes, his documents, and his calendar. I send myself anything of importance and delete everything. Before I leave, I'll have Rafe destroy the hard drive, though, just to be safe.

A rap on the door startles me from my thoughts.

"Come in," I chirp, a little too cheerful for a cartel queen. I do manage to pull the gun into my lap to hide it away in case it is anyone besides Rafe or Dad.

The door swings open and in strides a man. A scary yet handsome man. Black suit. Near black hair slicked back. Silvery scars crisscrossing all over his cheeks and forehead. His cheeks are smooth shaven and he wears a distinguished goatee that's been groomed neatly. When his pale brown eyes meet mine, a black eyebrow arches up in surprise.

"You must be Duvan's little play thing," he says smoothly.

I don't see any weapons in his possession, but I'm not stupid. I clutch the gun under my desk and expel a ragged breath. Three men file into the room behind him. All intimidating. Dangerous looking. All scowling.

"He preferred the term wife. You must be Dora's cousin," I grit out.

He regards me in confusion. "Who the hell is Dora?"

"Forget it," I utter. "Diego Gomez?"

He straightens his tie and saunters over to the desk. I

motion for him to sit. His eyes are all over my body, sizing me up. Once he decides I'm not a threat, he waves at his men. "Outside."

They don't argue. They step out and leave me alone with this slimeball.

"I must say, cariño," he utters as he drops down into the chair across from me, "you're not at all what I expected. You're nothing but a little girl."

My hackles rise and I straighten my back. "I'm little, I'll give you that." My voice drops to a whisper. "But you have no idea who I am or what I'm made of."

The threat hangs in the air as Diego scrutinizes me. After a long moment, he lets out a boisterous laugh that echoes off the walls. "Fucking adorable is what you are." He stands and begins nosily walking around the office. Touching artwork on the wall. Running his fingertip along the mahogany of the desk. Tipping over a binder on the back credenza behind me. I remain frozen in my spot. My hand sweats from holding the gun and I fear I'm going to have to use it. When he swivels the chair around, I let out a squeak of surprise. His strong hand finds my throat and he lifts me easily to my feet.

"You don't threaten me, bitch," he spits out, his eyes flickering with rage. "I'll fuck you over this desk like the useless whore you are. I take what I want, cariño."

With a growl, I shove the loaded gun against his hard dick. "Back it up before I make you *my* bitch."

His eyes widen in shock and he releases me. Slowly, he steps backward. As soon as he's stepped out of my reach, I glare at him. "I'm here to do business, asshole. Not let you take what belongs to me. Are you interested or am I selling to Camilo?"

He swallows and his body ripples with anger. "You're fucking feisty, bitch."

"Call me bitch again and I'm going to unload every bullet I've got into your cock and sorry ass balls," I snap. "Are we doing business or what?"

"I came here expecting to slap a whore around and instead, I meet you. No wonder Duvan gave his nuts to you. You probably fuck like a wild beast." His light brown eyes fall to my chest and he smirks. "I'd certainly like to have a go to see if I'm right." Despite having a loaded gun pointed at his junk, he's sporting a very large hard-on.

"Dream on, dick," I mutter. "How much are you offering?"

He rolls his eyes, as if I'm the annoying one here. He's the one who thinks he can stroll in, slap me around, fuck me, and then take what he wants. Over my dead body. "Three million pesos."

I almost laugh at him. I may be young and way out of my league and totally American, but I am not fucking stupid. "Nice try. We're talking good 'ol US dollars here. Not pesos. You and I both know this is worth a helluva lot more than a measly hundred grand."

His eyes widen in surprise once again. For a drug king, he sure does a piss poor job of hiding his thoughts. "I see. What did you have in mind?"

I know he wants me to throw out some over-the-top number as if I have no idea what I'm talking about. But I do. I've spent days learning of his properties, the value of the coke based on the amount we have in production, and all of his other assets.

"Twelve million."

His laugh is so loud that one of his men peeks in briefly to check on us. Once he closes the door and Diego sees I'm not kidding, his laughter dies. "No fucking lie. You are as smart as you are sexy. You sure you don't want to let Daddy Diego fuck your tight cunt. I'll put a ring on your finger if that makes you happy. What's one more wife?"

Bile rises in my throat, and I wish I'd have eaten more this morning than the two pieces of buttered toast. As soon as I get to California, I'm going to need to see a doctor to make sure I'm taking care of this baby properly.

"I don't want your dick," I tell him softly. "I just want your money."

He smirks. "You sure you don't want to be one of my wives? You sure as hell act like them."

I cringe wondering what it must be like married to this man. At least Duvan was good to me. He loved me and tried desperately to keep the dark parts of his business out of my sight.

"Twelve million. I want it wired to this account." I slide a handwritten piece of paper toward him. When he grabs my wrist, I have the urge to shoot him in the head, but I don't have to. He's simply inspecting my tattoo.

"Ten," he counters and lets go of my hand. Respect flickers in his eyes. I'm not some whore. I loved Duvan. He was my husband, and I won't let his hard work be stolen from us.

"Twelve, Diego."

His eyes flit to my chest. "Twelve and a blow job."

I roll my eyes. "No."

"Eleven and I see your tits."

"Jesus, you're a pig."

"You make me hard as fuck, cariño. I'm not leaving without seeing those pretty nipples."

I cross my arms over my chest. "You can forget it. Do we have a deal?"

He stands and reaches his hand across the desk. "Let me smell your cunt and the money is yours."

I gape at him for one long moment of hesitation, and it's a terrible mistake. He grabs me by the elbow in a brutal grip. His other hand is fast as he wrenches the weapon from my hand. With a growl, he drags me over the desk and papers hit the floor. I attempt to claw at him but before I know it, he has me twisted and pushed over the desk with both wrists in his grip. The mahogany is cold against my cheek.

"Help!" I cry out.

His laughter is cold. "My men have your men. Cariño, it's just us now."

Tears roll out when he presses his hardened cock against my ass. My wrists are locked in his strong hand and he uses the other one to stroke my hair. He fucking pets me like I'm a cat.

"So soft," he says with a growl.

"Please don't rape me," I beg. "I'm pregnant."

His grip on my hands loosens. "With Duvan's child?"

"Of course," I snarl.

He fingers a strand of my hair and gives it a gentle tug. "You'd be such a pleasure to tame."

"Please don't."

I'm so sure he's going to rape me that I start to mentally check out. I remain completely still for what feels like forever, praying to God he doesn't fuck me. But he doesn't fuck me. He just keeps me trapped as if I'm the pet he never was allowed to have as a child. I shiver when he presses a kiss to the back of my skull.

"I'm not a villain, cariño," he says in a firm tone as he releases my hands. He then gives me a playful slap to my ass before pulling away. "I'm a businessman. Now that I've gotten what I want, I'll give you what you want."

He helps pull me upright and steadies me on my feet. I'm in too much shock to do anything but gape at him. I'm disgusted by the sleaze but I don't dare do or say anything to set him off. He didn't rape me but it doesn't mean he won't. My hands tremble as he sifts through some papers on the floor. Eventually, he pulls up the wiring instructions and winks at me. Then, he stands before offering me back my gun.

"Luis!" he barks toward the door.

One of the scary men storms inside. His eyes never even glance over at me. Diego hands him the slip of paper.

"Make it happen."

Luis nods and pulls out his phone. A few moments later, the transaction is done. Once he proves it to me on the phone, he dismisses Luis.

"This office and everything in it, now belongs to me, cariño," he says with a growl. "Are you sure you want to stand there looking so fucking fine? Don't you have a flight to catch back to your pussy country? If you wait around any longer, I'll claim you too."

I start past him toward the door, but before I get to it, he once again grabs on to me. He takes the gun from me and shoves it into the back of his slacks. His light brown eyes are narrowed and he seems to inhale me. My heart rate is thundering right out of my chest.

"I'm leaving," I assure him.

His grip on my bicep tightens as he walks me toward the wall. Once my ass hits the drywall, I let out a yelp. He travels his gaze over my forehead, then my eyes, along my nose, lingers on my lips, before landing on my throat.

"This," he hisses as he clutches the necklace Ren gave me with Duvan's ring on it. "Is mine. As collateral."

I cry out when he yanks the chain, breaking it. A tear races down my cheek and I shake my head. "N-No. Please don't take that."

His black eyebrow lifts up in surprise. "Not so fearless, are you?"

"Why do you need collateral? I'm giving it to you. I'll sign over the deed. Just please don't take my necklace."

He pockets my jewelry and his lips lift up on one side. "You will sign over the deed. But I need to own something that you cherish, so that if Camilo loses his mind over our deal, I'll know how to get back in touch with you and that you'll listen. Once this all blows over, you can have it back. I promise, cariño."

I shake my head. "I can't let you take my jewelry. Anything else. Please."

His hand palms my stomach. "Anything?"

I'm seconds away from vomiting at his insinuation. He'll never get my child.

"I'm a very patient man. I could keep you until you give birth to this child and then keep the baby as collateral if you'd rather," he tells me, his voice low and threatening.

Another tear strolls down my cheek. He leans forward and kisses the wetness. "I didn't think so. I'll keep it safe. I promise." His suffocating presence pulls away from me. "Now you better go, little lady, before I change my mind. Letting you go is taking all of my self-control. I've been tempted by how sweet you are and I'm starved for a tiny little taste. My cock is dying to have the whole fucking buffet."

I shudder and stumble over to the door.

"Wait," he barks out. "Danilo!"

Another man walks into the office, this one dressed as nice as Diego, and carries a briefcase.

"We still have to sign a few things, cariño," he tells me. "My attorney will get them ready for us. Then you're free to go."

The next twenty minutes are torture. He won't quit staring at me as if he's going to eat me. And my heart aches knowing my husband's wedding ring sits in his pocket. I scribble my signature on the necessary documents all the while counting down the seconds until I can leave.

Once we're finished and his attorney stacks the papers in the briefcase, Diego regards me with a wolfish grin.

"Nice doing business with you, Gabriella Rojas. I never expected things to go so..." His words trail off as his gaze drops between my legs. "Beautifully."

I storm away from him toward the door. Once I wrench it open, I glare at him over my shoulder. "I want my ring back. I suggest you find a way to make that happen sooner rather than later."

"Ahh," he chuckles. "Another threat by the feisty little fox."

"It's tigress to you, asshole."

# VI | Brie

I'T'S BEEN A MONTH SINCE I SOLD MY SOUL TO THE DEVIL AT the tune of twelve million dollars. He hasn't messed with me anymore but he also still hasn't returned my ring. I've managed to finally sell the house and have liquidated the last of Duvan's assets.

Everything has gone well.

Too well, in fact.

And that keeps me on alert.

Camilo and Esteban are still nowhere to be found. Vee is still in hiding. I've been waiting for something bad to happen but each day is just another day. One more day further away from the last time I saw Duvan.

My belly is still small. I've finally started to get over my morning sickness. At least a little bit. Luciana gets me to eat and Daddy gets me to talk. After that day at the warehouse, I'd found my dad's beaten body lying beside our vehicle. Rafe was bleeding from his nose but wasn't in as bad of shape. I learned from Rafe that my father went crazy when he found out I was alone with Diego. They had to beat the hell out of him to keep him from interrupting our business.

I still never told him exactly what happened.

And I never will.

If he knew that Diego had been all over me and throwing out threats left and right, he'd have murdered that creep and brought the entire cartel's wrath down upon us. A shudder ripples through me. That will be a secret I keep to myself for as long as I live.

I walk through the now fairly empty house. Ren told me to ship the important stuff to his townhouse and that he'd keep up with it until I was ready to come for it. Everything else, we sold with the house.

Speaking of Ren, I haven't been able to get ahold of him for a few days. It is weird not to talk to him. After a month of Skyping every day, I feel isolated and all alone by not getting to hear his voice. Even if we don't really talk that much.

Tomorrow morning, Daddy, Luciana, and I have planned to fly out of Colombia. I'm equal parts sad and happy. On one hand, I'll be happy to leave the nightmare behind. But by leaving the nightmare, I'll also be abandoning my memories with Duvan. As much as I would rather stay and raise my baby in this house where we can feed the chickens every day, I know it isn't safe for my child. Not with people like Esteban and Diego lurking about.

In America, we can be free from all of this.

I push down my yoga pants and kick out of them. It's late and even though I'm not tired, I know I'll be exhausted on the trip tomorrow. I need to try and sleep at least. Duvan's old T-shirt swallows my small frame and my swollen bare breasts hang heavy beneath the fabric. I've outgrown all of my bras lately. I'll definitely have to do some shopping in California. I switch off the overhead light and am just crawling into our bed for the last time, when I hear a crash downstairs.

I scramble across the bed to the table where I keep a gun. I'll never feel one hundred percent safe, especially here, but the gun sure helps. Men are shouting downstairs. More crashing. On shaky legs, I slide off the bed and frantically look for a place to hide. I'm just darting toward the bathroom when I hear footsteps thundering up the stairs. My heart lurches in my throat. I freeze and instantly hate myself for not running. It's almost as if I'm waiting for…

The door swings open and a madman enters. Blood trickles from his bottom lip. The muscles in his neck are taut with tension. His brown hair is messy and overgrown. It hangs into his eyes, making him appear as though he's some untamed animal. His cheeks are scruffy and his jaw is sharp. The black Soundgarden T-shirt molds to his sculpted body. I'm frozen in shock, no longer in fear.

"Ren?"

"Your dad's an asshole," he utters, his hands fisted. He seems to snap out of his rage and his eyes skim over my clothing while his gaze softens. He wipes the blood away from his bottom lip with the back of his hand before he flashes me a grin I remember from when times were simpler. "Do I get a hug?" When our eyes meet again, a familiar glimmer flickers in his.

I jolt out of my shocked stance, set the gun down on the end table, and run over to him. He doesn't wait, stalking toward me to meet halfway. The moment he gathers me in his arms, I relax. I relax for the first time in over a month. All of my friends, aside from Luciana, have gone radio silent. All but *this* friend.

*This* friend is here.

Hugging me so tight, I think I might break.

Inhaling my hair as if I'm a delicate and rare rose.

Muttering out words of relief.

"Jesus," he utters, embracing me tighter. "It's been forever since I've hugged you."

I let out a laugh but it soon turns into tears. The relief is overwhelming, and I lose myself to it. Within seconds, I'm sobbing so hard, I think I might collapse. When my knees buckle, Ren slides his strong arm under my legs and lifts me. I cry against his chest, soaking his shirt as he carries me over to my bed. At first, I stiffen because if he crawls into this bed with me, it'll be his scent that replaces Duvan's. The thought terrifies me. But tomorrow it won't matter, anyway. I'll be gone. The idea of Ren holding me like old times seems to soothe my battered heart.

*His* scent is comforting too.

The springs groan in protest when Ren sets me down on the bed. He kicks off his shoes and scoots in beside me. As soon as he drags the covers over us, I clutch his T-shirt and bury my face against him. His fingers stroke through my hair. I cry for my loss. For the unfairness of this life. For the assaults I've suffered. The men who have abused me. I cry for my child who will never know its father. I cry for…me.

Ren, just like on our Skype sessions, doesn't speak. His strength speaks volumes. It steadies me. Roots me into the ground so I don't blow away in the wind. Like the gnarly branches of his tree tattoo, he holds me against his solid frame, keeping me safe from the awful world I know.

When my tears finally dry up and all that can be heard

is Ren's soft breathing, I look up at him. The lamp light casts dark shadows on his face. It's so different than I remember. Where is the smile that used to light up his whole face? Where are his blue eyes that would twinkle with delight when he saw me?

Ren is different, just like me.

He's seen unspeakable horrors. I've lived them.

He's teetered an impossible line with his sister. She stole from me.

He's lost his love. I've lost my love.

Our hearts have been slayed and left for dead.

The innocence we once knew has been obliterated. There's no collecting those pieces and putting them back together again.

"Did you and Daddy get in a fight?" I murmur in question.

His eyes that had been staring off toward the window find mine. A storm brews in his dark gaze. It makes me shiver. Thinking I'm cold, he pulls me tighter. Absently, he presses a kiss to my forehead and it stills my racing heart. "Your dad thought I was someone else. Three months ago, he'd have probably been able to gut my ass. Unfortunately for him, I've been spending a lot more time lifting than he has. We scuffled until he realized it was me, and that I wasn't coming here to kill you. Now he's downstairs on the phone with my dad, bitching."

A chuckle rumbles in my chest. Poor Daddy has done nothing but either kick ass or get his ass kicked since he came for me. He always looks so tired. I know he just wants to get back to California so he can have his life back again.

My smile falls.

Does that life involve me?

How can he have Hannah and I both?

The answer is…he can't.

I won't be able to see that woman without wanting to claw her eyeballs out.

"I wasn't expecting you to show up," I tell him after a few moments.

His fingers find my overgrown bangs and he tucks them behind my ear. "I could've waited a couple more days to see you, but I didn't want to. I also didn't think you travelling with a wanted felon was a good idea. The last thing you need is to get dragged to prison because you were in the wrong place at the right time."

My eyes find his—his gaze boring a hole through me. When did Ren become so intense? I reflect back on all the things I've dealt with in the past month. When did I become so intense? We're both strung so tight, we're sure to snap at any moment.

"Thank you for coming," I murmur. "I've been so lost and lonely. With Vee and Oscar gone too, I've been drifting. If it weren't for you, I'd have already lost my mind."

His brows furl together. He grits his teeth together as if he's holding in a mouthful of words. I want to pry his lips apart and pull them from him.

"What?" I ask.

He swallows. "I'm so fucking sorry, Brie."

Tears sting my eyes, but I quickly blink them away. "My life is a mess."

"I'm here now. I'll help you clean it all up. Your mess is mine." He leans forward and kisses the corner of my mouth. It stirs old feelings in my belly. "Go to sleep, Juliet. You've got a big day tomorrow."

I drift off, losing myself to nostalgic memories of when life was easy and fun. Before the cartel, before my dad came back, before Heath tried to ruin my life. Back when I was just a girl looking out a window, wishing for a boy to climb the tower and save me.

*"Tigress…"*

*I groan in protest. I'm too sleepy to get up.*

*"Tigress…"*

*"Mmmm," I grumble.*

*"Tigress…"*

My dreams tease me and bleed into reality. I hate that I can have him there and not in real life. Sometimes, when I wake up, his scent lingers. I can almost still hear his whispers against the shell of my ear. I'm oftentimes still wet from remembering the way he would touch me.

And now, in the pitch black of my bedroom, I'm once again taunted by his memory. He seems so real. I dance my fingertips along his bare chest. Solid muscle. Smooth contours and lines. So perfect.

My breasts ache to have him gripping them to the point of pain. I'd do anything to have his teeth on my nipples one last time. Greedy not to lose him in this moment, I regain full clarity and I straddle him. His cock is erect and at full attention.

God he feels so real.

"I missed you so much," I murmur in the dark, my fingernails raking along his chest.

His body tenses as if I've just woken him. Strong hands slide up my bare thighs and grip my hips just under my shirt. I want to glue them to me so he'll never let me go. Between the thin fabric of his boxers and my barely-there panties, I'm sure he can feel how wet I am as I rub against his throbbing cock. It's been so long.

"Brie…" His voice is all wrong but it's real. So fucking real.

"Shhh," I tell him, needing the fantasy to remain. Reality is a goddamned bitch.

He lets out a low growl and his thumbs dig into my flesh. I rock against him almost painfully. My body needs this release. I grab on to his muscular shoulders so I can stabilize myself. Grinding against him feels so good. So perfect.

Tendrils of pleasure begin lazily making their way through my veins as if they've suddenly awoken from a long slumber. Much like the bliss of the heroin I once loved, I quiver with anticipation as it snakes its way through me, leaving a delicious sting in its wake. My pussy throbs with need. It won't be long before I come.

And like so many nights before, I'll reawaken with a pillow between my legs. My fantasy nothing more than a sad dream. But it never stops me from giving in to these dreams. I greedily steal them each time.

His hands grip the bottom of my T-shirt and he starts to drag it up my body. Reality is hiding just beyond the door of my mind. Reminding me this isn't real. That he's not real. That my fantasy is an imposter.

I turn my back on that door.

Lifting my arms, I let him tug the shirt from me. His palms slide to my swollen breasts and he squeezes them.

Admires them. Gets used to the new size of them. He sits up on the bed until our stomachs press together. His hot mouth finds my nipple. So tentative at first but then he suckles on it. Bites it. Draws pleasure from such a small area just with his mouth. My panties are drenched.

This isn't enough.

I need more.

So much more from him.

Raking my fingers through his hair, I blatantly ignore the fact that his hair is different. I don't get caught up in reality. This fantasy is mine. I'll live in it forever.

He grips my ass to the point I know I'll be bruised. His need to consume me—to tear me apart—has me flying higher and higher toward ecstasy.

"I need you," I whisper so quietly I don't think he hears.

But then his hot breath is between my breasts, sending chills down my spine. "I'm not him."

*I'm not him.*

A tear streaks down my cheek and I shake my head. "Shhh."

When I grind into him hard, he lets out a sound of pure bliss. But then his hands are in my hair almost painfully. He jerks my head back so that my breasts jut right into his face. His teeth drag along my flesh before he sinks them into my skin. I cry out in pain—but it's pain mixed with pleasure, and I need it. "I'm not him, baby."

I slap my hand over his mouth so he'll shut up. This seems to spark a reaction from him because he flips us around and presses me into the bed. His strong hands grab my wrists as he jerks them above my head. My legs are still spread apart. He never loses our stride and continues rubbing against me in a way that has me so close to climaxing.

I just need to hold on to the fantasy a moment longer.

Then I can hate myself all I want.

Then I can force myself to face the truth.

Then I can apologize.

"I'm not him," he growls in a no-nonsense way. He grips my chin almost brutally before crashing his lips to mine. This kiss tastes familiar, but the harsh way he delivers it isn't familiar. Despite not recognizing it, I crave it.

"I need you inside me," I plead, hot tears rolling from my eyes. I'm fully aware of my betrayal but I won't let it win. Not now.

"Jesus fucking Christ!" he hisses.

At one time, he'd have been the gentleman. Made me come to terms with reality. Held me through what I'd almost done.

But this isn't the boy I remember. I don't know this man at all. I let out a sigh of relief when he lifts up long enough to pull his cock from his boxers. My panties are hastily pushed to the side. There isn't any time to change my mind. To focus on the wrongness. To erase this mistake.

With one painful thrust, he's deep inside me, drawing out a crushing wail. His cock splits me wide open all the way down to my soul. Flashes of a simple past flit through my mind like blinding white zaps. Each one electrocuting me with realization. This isn't my fantasy at all, and yet I'm soaking it all in. Drawing comfort from the sound of the waves. The warm sunshine. The way he used to kiss me until my mouth was raw on the beach. How we'd dry hump long before he took my virginity.

His fingers are back to biting into my jaw as he kisses me.

There's nothing soft about the way he mauls me. He thrusts into me so hard, I imagine I'll be bruised. My clit throbs out of control each time his body hits mine.

So close…

*Don't think about it, just do it,* I tell myself.

I make the mistake of opening my eyes. Moonlight peeks in through the window, casting a sliver of light across his face. One steely blue eye is illuminated and it bores into me. His one eye flashes with anger and love and need. And it's too much.

I want to run away from it all.

Pretend this never happened.

"Goddammit, Brie," he growls. "Look at me."

His fierce command has my eyes popping back open and my pussy clenching in response. His gaze softens before he kisses me in a gentler way. A way I remember. A way I used to dream about late at night before my world turned upside down.

"Relax, baby," he murmurs against my lips. "Just let it go."

I shut off my mind and allow my orgasm to overtake me. My nerve endings take on life as they all seem to explode at once. The shudder that wracks through me is so strong, I actually jerk from beneath him. When my body clamps down around his, he lets out a guttural groan. A gush of his hot seed fills me. Throb after exhilarating throb.

"What have I done?" I whisper mostly to myself.

He releases his grip on my wrists and slides a palm over my heart. "You were letting go of some of the pain."

I blink in the darkness, stunned by his words. My body is relaxed. My mind is calm. It's just my heart that is destroyed. I feel like a whore who can't keep her legs closed.

"My heart still belongs to him," I blurt out.

He flinches at my words. But then he takes my tattooed wrist and draws it to his lips. The way he kisses it reminds me of how Duvan would. It makes my chest ache painfully. "I know, Brie. Nobody's asking you to forget about him. But having that orgasm was probably the best thing you could do for yourself right now. You were so fucking tense."

He slips his softened cock out of me and then climbs off the bed. Soon, the bathroom light blinds me. It sheds light on the horror of what I've just done. When he returns, carrying a wet cloth, I can't bear to look at him.

"Brie."

I clench my eyes closed, hoping he'll get a clue.

"Open your eyes, dammit." His words are harsh and it makes me open them so I can see his expression. He's never been the angry type. I don't understand who he is anymore.

"I'm sorry," I whisper.

He grabs my panties and tugs them down my thighs. They're soaked with his cum and need to go. He clutches my knees and pulls me open once he's removed the last of my clothing. I start to drag my knees back together, but he's stronger and he wins. The warm cloth travels over my still pulsating clit as he cleanses me between my thighs. He does it in such a gentle, protective way, I think I might burst into tears. My emotions are all over the place. When he's finished, he stalks back over to the bathroom. I get a better peek at his back tattoo, which seems to have a lot more going on with it since my last perusal. Thankfully, he's pulled his boxers back into place.

"You didn't do anything wrong," he tells me as soon as the room goes dark again. I should probably make moves to find my shirt or a new pair of panties or a wall to put between us. Instead, I remain frozen.

He slips into the bed and hauls me to him. His sculpted chest presses firmly against my back while his arm wraps possessively around me. Now that I'm fully aware of my situation, it's more brutal to my psyche admitting that I need him comforting me right now. If I could fall asleep forever like this and never wake up, I would.

His lips kiss my shoulder, and I shiver. I don't know what to do. I should push him away and yet I don't. I should ask him to sleep elsewhere and yet I don't. I should warn him I'll only fuck up his heart because I'm a mess and yet I don't.

I let him hold me.

I let him kiss my neck.

I let him snuggle his flaccid cock against my ass.

I'll allow myself this one night. Then, tomorrow, with reality, I can deal with the consequences of my actions. Right now, though, I refuse to let them win.

For the first time in over a month, I fall asleep with a blank mind.

My heart aches but not as much as usual.

Tonight, for a short while, I am free.

# PART TWO:

"Even Though Our Love Is Doomed" by Garbage

# VII | Ren

I'VE SLEPT LIKE SHIT FOR MONTHS. MY MIND HAS BEEN plagued by all the wrongs and I can't focus on anything right. Everything seemed to be spiraling out of control.

Until now.

Sleeping with Brie tucked in against my chest was calming. The anger that had been simmering below my surface seemed to cool. For once in what seems like forever, I slept easily.

But last night?

Last night was probably a big fucking mistake. As much as I wanted to be inside of her, it was wrong. She was lying to herself and wanted me to play along with her little charade.

I fucking did.

Fucked her right into a sleepy stupor.

Her scent still clings to me and my dick twitches to ram into her again. Her body simply responded so differently than the other two times we'd had sex. It wasn't lovemaking, like before. It was carnal, animalistic, unapologetic fucking.

And, my God, it was amazing.

But now she's locked herself in the bathroom. As soon as her alarm went off, she bolted from the bed, and out of my arms, to lock herself away from the reality of what we'd done.

I need to make her understand it wasn't a mistake.

It was simply…a release.

A release she needed more than I did.

With a sigh, I climb out of bed and walk over to the window. The sky is overcast and ominous as a storm looms. I catch sight of my reflection in the glass. My eyebrows are furled together in a contemplative manner. The stubble on my cheeks has grown in recently. I'm normally one to keep my face clean-shaven, but lately, I like the way it scratches my palm when I'm in one of my moods. Tiny bites of pain keep me alive.

I wonder if they could keep her alive too.

Would the hair scratch her inner thighs in a way that hurts so good?

Finding my jeans, I pull them up quickly and forgo a shirt. When I make it over to the bathroom door, I raise my hand to knock but pause when I hear her sniffling inside.

"Brie," I murmur, "open up."

The sink turns on and then, after a moment, she opens the door. Her face is splotchy and red from crying. But it's the hollow look in her brown eyes that's haunting.

"What I did…what we did…" Her bottom lip wobbles as tears well in her pretty eyes.

Stalking over to her, I grip her chin and tilt her head up so I can look at her. The tears break free from her eyelids and race each other down her cheeks. Her two eyebrows are pinched together as if she's in pain.

I caused this pain.

But I can take it away too.

"Nobody is judging," I tell her firmly. "Nobody." When I hug her to me, she doesn't resist. Instead, she clings to my bare chest and cries. Brie has always been so strong. It's a hidden strength that not many see. I've always seen it, though. Seen the fierce glint in her eyes when she'd talk about her future. And when she was with Duvan, her strength seemed to intensify. He was good for her. I'll always be grateful for the love he gave her when not many people would. It was a love she needed—something I couldn't quite give to her at the time.

One day, I will find exactly what she needs and I will give it to her.

My heart. My soul. My devotion.

Of course, now's not the time. What she needs from me now is my strength. This poor woman is broken and slayed. She's bleeding uncontrollably from a wound in her heart.

I'm going to help her soothe the pain.

I'll wrap her up tight in my safe, loving heart and keep her protected from the hurt that plagues her.

"I'm going to be sick," she hisses a second before jerking from my embrace.

She clambers over to the toilet and barely pushes the lid open before she's puking inside. I storm over to her and grab a handful of her hair to keep it from her face. Between her heaves, she sobs so loudly, I'm sure God can hear. I hope he hears her pain and fucking does something about it. I hope he gives her some peace.

Once she's done throwing up, I release her to get a cold, wet cloth. She still hugs the toilet bowl but has shifted to sit on her ass.

"I'm going to get you something to drink," I tell her.

I stalk out of the bathroom and through her bedroom on a mission to the kitchen. The rest of the house is dark and quiet. But when I reach the kitchen, Gabe sits perched on a bistro chair. His hair is disheveled. A dark, black circle rings his eye where I managed to get a swing in on him last night.

While I can respect his need to protect Brie, I wasn't going to be deterred.

When he notices me, his tired brown eyes meet mine. The usual anger doesn't flicker in them. Sadness does.

"How's Brie?" he mumbles before sipping from his mug of black coffee. His gaze rakes over my bare chest. I'm sure he knows we've been intimate but I don't give a rat's ass what he thinks about it.

"She'll be fine. A little sick this morning," I grunt back as I rummage in some cabinets on a hunt for crackers. The house is all packed up, but I do find a basket of snacks on the counter.

"How am I going to fix this, Ren?" His voice is choked. Broken. Vulnerable even.

I pluck a sleeve of peanut butter crackers from the basket before regarding him. "Fix what?"

He runs his fingers through his messy hair. "Your sister. My daughter. How do I get to have this family? My family? Together. Under one roof."

Just the mention of my sister has my blood boiling. "You chose Hannah over Brie. I don't understand how. She certainly doesn't."

He flinches at my words. With a scowl, he twists his wedding ring on his finger. "Love is fucking messy."

Tell me about it.

"You can't have the best of both worlds," I finally utter out. "You want true love and children with Hannah but then you have this amazing daughter too. Unlike most normal blended families, they can't be around each other, because Hannah is a fucking murderer. She killed your daughter's mother. So, Gabe, I'm sorry, man, but you're just going to have to accept that you can't have both. You can't fix it."

He clenches his eyes shut and lets out a ragged sigh. "Toto would love Brie. You know she would."

Toto's pretty brown eyes are at the forefront of my mind. I love that kid like you would not believe. "Brie will love her too. With time. You can't rush into it, though. Maybe one day I can bring Toto with me to visit her. Brie is a good person," I tell him vehemently. "She has so much love in her heart. It's just been crushed in the past few years. Once she begins to heal again, I think she'll be ready to show some of that love."

He stares at me for a long moment. "You're okay, kid."

I let out a humorless chuckle as I snag one of the last cans of Sprite from the refrigerator. "I'm not a kid anymore, man. I kicked your old ass last night."

His lips tug into a smile. "You caught me at a weak moment. Next time, your ass is mine."

I smirk and flip him off before trotting back to Brie's room. She's still in the bathroom on the floor where I left her. Kneeling beside her, I pop open the Sprite and help her take a sip. When she notices the crackers, her nose scrunches up.

"I don't think I can eat anything," she murmurs.

I stroke her hair and set the drink on the counter. "You need to if you want to feel any better. When my mom was pregnant with Mason, she did okay as long as we kept food in her. It was when her stomach was empty that she would get sick."

She turns and regards me with sad brown eyes. If I could cut open my own chest and give her my beating heart, I would. If only somehow that would fill her empty one up. I sit beside her so that I'm facing her.

"Tell me about…" I trail off as I clutch her shaking hand. I draw it toward me so I can look at her tattoo. "Him."

Her eyes snap to mine and she frowns. "You want to know about him? I thought you hated him."

Bringing her wrist to my mouth, I kiss the flesh there, my eyes never leaving hers. "He made you happy. How could I hate him for that?"

Tears pool in her eyes and she breaks our gaze. For a moment, I don't think she'll speak, but then she does.

"He was good to me. Found ways to make me laugh. Wanted me to make my own decisions. He paid attention to the small details, and sometimes I thought maybe he knew me better than I knew myself. Duvan filled parts of me I didn't know were empty." Her lips curve up on one side, and I see a small flash of a smile. "He encouraged me to be a better person. Loved me without rules or conditions. He was so excited to be a father." Her voice cracks and her tears fall freely down her cheeks. "We were going to have such a good life together."

I squeeze her hand. "But it was stolen from you."

That day online, when I watched as Heath appeared behind the finally-happy woman and her husband, will forever be etched into my brain. I've never been so fucking terrified in my life. The scene unfolded like that of a horror movie, but it was real. Every single awful second was real. Their love, so visible on the screen was literally cut open and drained before my very eyes. I was disgusted to see something so beautiful ruined because of the greed of another. Heath had vacant eyes as he slit open Duvan's throat. Her screams had been otherworldly as her love died in her arms. I still remember how Oscar tried desperately to shield Vee from the gruesome scene—a scene her father played a leading role in, and his brother the victim. And just when I thought I'd lose Brie next to a brutal rape and murder, Gabe showed up. Too little, too late, though. It'll be a guilt he'll have to bear on his shoulders until the day he dies. How he wasn't quick enough to get to them. To save Duvan. Watching Gabe stab Heath to death was oddly satisfying. If I were there, I'd have wanted to do it myself. Duvan was always the better man when it came to the two of us in Brie's eyes, but I never once wished him dead.

Because his death meant the death of her heart.

And her heart has always been my focus.

"Your mother would have liked Duvan, huh?" I ask as I pull some tissue off the roll to dab her cheeks with.

She nods and gives me a brief wobbly smile. "Daddy would have hated him but Mom would have thought he was perfect." Her eyes flit to mine and an apology flickers in them. She has nothing to be sorry for.

"Why would your dad have hated him? Besides the fact that he hates everyone, of course," I say in a light tone.

She laughs through her tears. "He does hate everyone." Her finger brushes against the scab on my lip from where he split it with his fist. "Including you."

"After the black eye I gave him, I can agree with that." I wink at her.

Her smile falls and she regards me with a serious

expression. "Actually, Daddy would have hated the life I was exposed to with Duvan. We'd made a plan to get away from it all but for a while there…" she trails off and nervously starts to open the crackers.

I know she's thinking of what Esteban did to her. The drugs. The rape. The terror.

"Duvan may have led a dangerous life," I admit, "but your safety was his main priority. You were loved, Brie."

You're still loved.

She starts to cry, so I wrap my arms around her and haul her to me. For what seems like forever, we sit on the bathroom floor in an emotional embrace. When I hold her like this, I feel like I can keep the broken parts of her held together. That maybe, even if only for a moment, she'll feel whole again.

"I'm so lost," she murmurs against my chest. "I'm drifting. No home. No future. No anything. I don't even know who I am anymore. I'm sinking, Ren, and it feels like I'll never hit the bottom."

I kiss the top of her head. "I've got you. You may feel lost or alone, but you're not. I'm right behind you. When you feel like falling, I will catch you."

She lifts her chin and peers up at me. Her swollen lips are so goddamned kissable, but I refrain. "I'm so scared."

Using my thumb, I swipe away a drying tear. "Even the bravest, toughest of people have moments of weakness. You're going to lick these wounds and then you're going to come out swinging." I smile at her. "You have his child inside of you. And that baby is going to need its mother to be strong."

Hope, such a rarity in her world, flickers in her eyes as if she believes every single word coming out of my mouth. My chest swells with happiness. I hope she hears them. Draws them inside her tattered heart and puts them on a shelf so she can stare at them. I mean every single word.

"You're going to cry it out," I tell her firmly. "And then you're going to sharpen those claws. The world is about to hear you roar, baby."

"Where do you want to go?" I ask as I toss the last of her and Luciana's bags into the back of my truck.

Brie glances over at Gabe, who is pacing beside my truck in the parking lot. When her eyes find mine again, she seems stressed. Probably wondering where the fuck she will go. Her dad seems confused on what to do as well. Talk about a clusterfuck.

"I'm taking her with me," Gabe says finally, his menacing gaze boring into me. "The girls are coming with me. I'll make it work."

Brie tenses and it's all I need. "Nope, old man. Remember, you have Hannah Bananas. They can stay at my place for the time being."

Gabe growls like a big grizzly bear but it doesn't faze me.

"Brie," he utters and stalks over to her. "I'll find a way for this to work. Just give me some time." He pulls her into a tight embrace, but she doesn't hug him back.

"Goodbye, Daddy."

He reluctantly lets her pull away from his hug. I give him a shrug of my shoulders as both women climb into the truck. Once they close the door, he storms toward me. His eyes are manic. I can tell he's losing his mind over the whole ordeal. I'd almost feel sorry for him, but I don't.

I feel sorry for Brie.

He had a hand in doing this to her.

My sister did this to her.

If anyone fixes things for her, it'll be me. I'm probably one of the few people she will let help her.

"Make sure she stays safe, Ren," he grumbles. "My baby girl needs protection. If she won't let me, then it has to be you."

"I'll never let anyone hurt her," I vow. My eyes narrow and my jaw clenches. The air seems to crackle with my heart-felt promise. "Now go see your *other* daughter. She needs you too."

Without waiting for a response, I stride over to the driver's side of the truck and hop in. Both women are somber. The entire ride to the townhouse is silent. Brie sits in the back seat. Occasionally our gazes meet in the mirror. When I finally pull into my neighborhood, Brie perks up and stares at all the modest townhomes. I liked this neighborhood because the homes were newer, but not gigantic, and fairly affordable compared to others in the area. And the best part is that it's within walking distance of the ocean.

I pull into the driveway next to Calder's black Tahoe and shut off the truck. "You both are welcome to stay for as long as it takes for you to get back on your feet," I say, making sure to look at both of them. "We have an extra bedroom. If you can deal with Calder eating all the food and leaving the toilet seat up, I think you'll be okay."

We all get out of the truck. Brie shields her eyes against the sun as she looks down the street. Between the townhouses, you can see the ocean. A salty breeze whips around us. Brie's T-shirt flaps in the wind, and it almost seems as if a gust will catch her just right and blow her away from me.

I would find her again.

I always do.

When she turns to look at me, she's wearing a small smile. Small smiles eventually lead to breathtaking ones. I'll take them all. "I like it here."

"Good." I flash her and Luciana a grin. "Let's get your stuff inside. Calder may eat a lot but he's actually a pretty decent cook. I texted him from the airport to tell him we'd be hungry."

They both trail inside behind me. The house is a little messy, because two bachelors aren't exactly good house-keepers, but it's still a nice place. I'm only renting for now. I'd wanted to buy, but Dad asked me to wait. Said it had nothing to do with the money I would spend from my trust fund but everything to do with the fact that I should wait before I plant my roots. Something about his words had halted me from making such a huge decision, like buying a house.

The place smells good. Calder's obsessed with Italian food and cooks it a lot. With Dad being vegan, we ate some pretty bland stuff growing up. It would seem my brother is as far from vegan as one could get.

"We're here," I holler as I waltz into the kitchen. My brother stands at the stove in nothing but a pair of jeans that barely stay on his ass and a blue beanie on his head. He's not wearing a shirt because, let's face it, he's Calder and he never wears a shirt. I smirk when I notice he's gotten yet another tattoo. Unlike my tats that make sense to me and are large pieces, he has a bunch of random shit all over his chest and arms. Mom knows about my tattoos but she would kill his ass if she saw his. Calder is still her baby boy despite being eighteen now and also having Mason on the scene.

"You kids hungry?" he questions, turning his gaze our way.

I roll my eyes when I see he's wearing a fucking *Blue's Clues* beanie. Where does he find this shit to taunt me with? He's beaming at me like the cat that ate the goddamned canary. That is, until his gaze falls behind me. When his smile falters, I assume it's because he sees how broken my Brie is. But when I turn, I realize his focus has landed somewhere else.

"Remember Luciana from when we visited? I know we weren't there very long, and she didn't come out much…" I glance up at my brother. A storm brews in his eyes before he seems to shake it away, replacing the odd look with one of smug assholeness, which he wears so well.

"Hey, Luci." He winks at her before going back to stir his sauce.

Luciana's face grows bright red. Her eyes remain on my brother's muscled body as he cooks. Maybe he'll stop obsessing so much over Vee and give some other chicks a chance. One can only hope.

"While he finishes up, I'll show you to your room," I tell the girls. Brie's face is impassive. I've seen the look on her face a thousand times over the past three years.

Block out the pain.

Focus on what's right in front of her.

Force a smile when necessary.

Deny tears from falling.

She's so fucking strong all the time. In those rare moments

85

when she breaks, I get to see down to her fragile core. I don't *want* her to have to be strong all the time. I want to be strong for her, so for once, Brie can relax.

"This is the guest room." I motion toward the neutrally decorated room. "The bed is big enough for the both of you, but if you don't want to sleep together, I can always take the couch and one of you can take my bed."

Brie sets her bags down and walks over to me. "Can I talk to you for a second?"

My hand finds the small of her back. She lets me guide her down to the master bedroom. Once we push inside the door and close it behind us, she turns her sad gaze to mine. Confusion and heartache storm behind her eyes. I can tell she wants to say something but simply doesn't have the words yet.

"Brie—"

"Can I sleep here tonight?" she blurts out.

Our eyes meet and shame washes over her features. Her bottom lip quivers and she bites it to keep it from moving. I want to bite it too. Like last night when I marked her perfect tit with my teeth.

"Of course you can," I tell her with a smile. "Like I said, I can take the couch and—"

"No," she interrupts. "*With* you." Her eyes close and her nose turns pink as she desperately fights her tears. "I just want to be held again."

I stalk over to her and pull her against my chest. Her rigid frame relaxes in my grip. "Brie, I will hold you until you don't want me to hold you anymore. Don't ever feel bad for wanting that."

Her head tilts up and she swallows. Pain hides in her eyes. I wish I could reach inside of her and patch it all up. I'm dying to heal every infliction she's ever suffered. "Hug buddies," she says softly, a false chuckle following.

Sliding my palms to her cheeks, I hold her face so I can stare deeply into her chocolate eyes. "And other kind of buddies too. Like last night. If that's what you need."

Her cheeks blaze red. "T-That was a mistake," she stammers out.

I run my thumb across her bottom lip, staring for just a moment at how her flesh resists and pulls with it. "Taking away some of your pain, if only for one night, was not a mistake. It was necessary."

# VIII | Brie t

THE SEMI COLD SHOWER DID NOTHING TO COOL THE flames of embarrassment that had painted my skin earlier. I'd basically, in a moment of desperation, begged Ren to let me sleep in his bed. My emotions have been chaotic for the past month. The only time I've felt even remotely okay was last night with his heavy arm wrapped across my middle.

I'm selfish because I want it again.

I want to close my eyes and feel safe.

Running a brush through my wet hair, I wonder how to navigate my messy world. I'd told Ren I was lost...and I am. The feeling isn't far off from when I was holed up in the basement with Esteban. I was drifting and alone. I never thought I'd be found again.

Thank God for Ren showing up when he did. He grounded me. I had begun to spin slightly out of control and he slowed the dizzying movement. Brought it to a screeching halt.

"Beh."

Luciana's brown eyes meet mine in the foggy mirror. She looks pretty with her hair hanging down in long waves in front of her face. She usually has it pulled back into a bun. It's weird seeing her look so casual.

"Everything okay?" I question.

She looks over her shoulder to the doorway and then back at me. Quickly, she nods her head but her cheeks light up in a pink hue.

"What's going on?"

With a frustrated huff, she pulls her phone from her pocket. Her long fingers fly across the keys. Seconds later, she hands me the phone that's pulled up to the Notes app.

**He looks like Justin Bieber!**

Frowning, I lift my gaze to meet hers. "Who?"

She grunts and steals the phone back. Then hands it back to me.

**Calder. OMG, did you see his chest? His muscles are huge. I want to lick them!**

At this, I burst out laughing. That girl has Bieber Fever bad. The fact that she thinks Calder looks like him has me quite amused. I personally don't see it, but Luciana seems convinced.

"Have you ever actually licked anyone's muscles before?" I ask with a lifted eyebrow.

Her gaze falls to the floor and she shakes her head. She taps away on the phone until she has a new message for me.

**I was a virgin until two summers ago. :(**

Her expression has lost the joviality from moments ago.

"Esteban?" I can hardly say his name without wanting to throw up.

Luciana nods and taps away some more.

*Yes. Esteban. He is the only one. He let his friends touch me sometimes but never let them do more.*

Memories of him assault me. The spaghetti we ate earlier is threatening to make a reappearance.

"I'm sorry," I mutter. "Getting fucked against your will doesn't count. One day, I hope you get to learn the difference with someone you care about."

She stares at me for a long moment, before her fingers type away at another message.

*Don't be sad, Brie.*

I close my eyes. Flashes of the way the heroin numbed me taunt me. Truth be told, I loved the feeling. How it made my pain disappear. How I faded into oblivion. Not a day goes by where, at some point, I don't physically crave it.

"I'm not feeling so hot," I lie when I reopen my eyes. "I'll see you tomorrow."

She gives me a quick hug and pecks my cheek before leaving. I shakily make my way over to the bed and sit. After dinner, Ren went to the basement to work out. He's been gone a couple of hours, and I wish he'd come back. At least when he's here, my mind clears some. I'm not trapped in a drug-in-duced haze in that basement or holding together my dead husband's neck.

I'm in the present.

The door clicks closed and I snap my attention over to it. Ren stands in the doorway looking too good for the way I feel. My hormones are all over the place. And right now, see-ing him all sweaty in nothing but a pair of low-slung basket-ball shorts and tennis shoes, enables my mind to lose focus on all my stress, and instead, hone in on him.

At one time, I used to sit in my window and stare at him

for hours. I loved how he'd drip with sweat, all of his muscles glistening. Now, he's larger and his skin is more colorful. He's the same boy and yet he's also this man.

A distracting man.

"You okay?" he asks as he kicks off his shoes. His eyebrows are pinched together in concern.

I nod and scoot further up the bed toward the headboard. His bed smells just like he always does. Leather and soap and safety. An odd yet extremely satisfying combination. His eyes travel along my bare legs before he clears his throat and turns his back to me as he heads toward the shower.

Once I hear the water turn on, I slip under the covers. My entire body is on edge. The dead organ that once beat in my chest has turned to stone. Each time I think of Duvan, another piece of it chips away. The only solution I have to keep it from whittling down to nothing is to completely shut out those parts. When Ren held me early this morning in my bathroom, I'd wanted to lock my mind down. Instead, he started asking questions. Drew out answers from me about my love for Duvan. It was therapeutic, in a way, but now that it's just me again, I don't want to be alone with my devastation.

My nerve endings seem to pulsate with energy. Each time I close my eyes, Duvan's purple-black irises shine back at me. It hurts so fucking badly to think about him. I dig my fingernails into my palms and attempt to drive away the pain.

I'm not sure how long I remain in this position, but it isn't until the overhead light above me is shut off that I finally drag myself from my inner torture chamber. A warm body slides into the bed beside me. I let out a relieved groan when he hauls me into his arms.

He smells so good.

Clean and strong.

Ren.

"You're crying," he says softly. "What can I do to help?"

I didn't even realize I was crying. When my fingertips touch my cheek, I feel the wetness there. "I don't know."

"Were you thinking about him?" he murmurs, his fingers stroking the flesh on my upper arm.

"Always."

"I'm sorry this happened to you. It's not fair. You of all people deserved better."

I choke out my words. "I don't want to talk right now," I whisper. "I just need…" My fingertips lightly skate down his sculpted chest toward his stomach. In the dark, his physique reminds me of Duvan's.

The smells are all wrong.

The voice is all wrong.

But the heat rippling from him is all right.

By the time my palm reaches his shorts, his cock is erect and straining against the fabric. Last night, he split me apart with pleasure. With every stroke and thrust, he drove away my sadness. It was fleeting but for a while, I was high.

Just like the heroin once did for me.

I was able to blur out all the heartache and focus on something nice for just a moment. Something that didn't destroy me, but instead, fulfilled me.

"I need you," I utter. "You're my distraction."

I hate myself for using Ren. For literally turning out the lights on our friendship to gain a high from his body. His warmth. His companionship. His pleasure. When daylight returns, I'll once again regret my actions. I'll detest my decision-making skills. Hate how weak I am.

Yet, right now, I don't care about any of that.

In the darkness, I crave the real life ecstasy that surges through my veins when I'm touched in just the right way. When his hot breath tickles the tender flesh along my throat. When his teeth bite me in a way that hurts so good.

"You're going to just keep pretending?" he asks, his lips pressing soft kisses below my ear.

My fingers find his still wet hair. "It's easier that way."

In the dark, I'm free to say whatever I want.

"Do you imagine it's him here instead of me?" He's not angry. At least I can't tell if he is. He sounds curious. As though he's trying to figure me out.

"Sometimes."

An animalistic sound rumbles from him tickling my throat as he trails south toward my chest. His palm cups my breast in an almost reverent way. But then his teeth are on my still tender nipple. He's not gentle as he sucks and nips at it. The contrast between his rough handling of one breast and his worshipping way of the other has me squirming beneath him. When he bites me once more, I dig my fingernails into his shoulder. A hiss escapes him. I expect him to move along but he bites me over and over, causing me to cry out and claw him again.

"I can see why he called you tigress," he murmurs against my sore nipple before kissing my skin softly. He suckles the flesh until he gets to my stomach. My pussy is throbbing with anticipation. The idea of having his lips on me between my thighs has my entire body thrumming with excitement.

In the dark, I'm transfixed in this moment.

Sadness and despair and regret aren't haunting me.

I'm lost in the best possible way.

My attention is torn away from my inner thoughts and is honing in on his lips. So soft. So tender. So loving. He kisses me just below my belly button. His palm splays across my midsection, which is beginning to soften and expand. He whispers something against my belly that I can't hear, but I feel. *So hot.*

"What did you say?" I question, my body practically twitching with the need to have him tear me apart.

His tongue flicks out and he drags it down my skin—lower and lower until he reaches my panty line just above my pubic bone. I'm so wet for him. If he were to touch my panties, he'd feel just how wet. His teeth find the fabric and he playfully tugs at it. I let out a mewl of pleasure when his thumb rubs along my clit through my panties to the part of me that practically drips with need.

"So wet," he says with a smug tone.

"What did you say before?" I ask again.

"I said, 'You're going to love your mom. Everyone does.'"

I'm stunned stupid, realizing he just spoke to my unborn baby. My entire body shivers from head to toe. His strong hands find my panties and he jerks them from my body. I am still thinking of his words until his nose rubs against my clit, sending fire shooting through me.

He's going to burn me alive from the inside out.

"Oh, God!" I cry out, my hips lifting to seek his mouth.

I'm not forced to wait much longer because a second later, his lips and tongue are all over my pussy. Tasting and sucking and licking and biting. So much sensation. Too much. But I need it all. I'm greedy, and it's addicting. The pleasure surging through me is better than any drug. His breath scorches my sensitive skin as he whispers sweet things against my flesh.

I hear those words and lock them up inside of me for safe keeping. Tuck them away in a memory box of my mind to open up and look at later when it's no longer dark.

"You're dripping for me, baby," he growls against my pussy. "I want to devour you all night long. Feast on this perfect part of you."

His hungry words only serve to drive me crazier than I already feel. I grip his hair when he starts to make good on his promise to consume me. My entire body—which had felt like an empty shell not even twenty minutes ago—comes alive. I jolt and squirm and cry out with every flick of his tongue. I beg and plead for I don't know what until he gives it to me. His teeth find my clit and he tugs. It hurts for just a moment until he sucks away the pain. I'm dizzy with the assault of sensations blasting through me from where his mouth is connected to me.

An orgasm with the ferocity and sudden onset like that of an unexpected tornado rips through me and decimates everything in its path.

"Ren!"

He jerks away from my throbbing sex and pushes my thighs apart. I let out a needy whine when I feel the head of his cock rubbing against my slick opening. Thankfully, he doesn't tease me, and instead drives into me with one hard thrust. My fingernails dig into his arms as he bucks into me like a savage beast. I like him like this.

Uncontrolled.

Hungry.

An animal who's starved only for me.

Possessive.

"Say it again," he orders, his voice deep and authoritative.

The echoes of it rumble their way straight to my core. "Nobody has to hear it but us."

"Ren," I murmur so softly, I wonder if he even hears it.

His mouth crashes against mine and we kiss unlike any time before. This kiss is greedy. Soul consuming. Two people with needs only the other can fulfil.

I want to touch every part of him as he fills me. To dance my fingers over his flesh and memorize each contour. Deep in my heart, I want to imagine it's Duvan taking me. But even as I think those words, I know they aren't one hundred percent true.

Ren isn't one I can simply block out.

He loves too hard. With such loyalty. It never waivers. A love that one can lean upon during life's biggest storm and not get blown away.

Here in the dark, I don't have to hide *from* Ren and pretend. It's now that I actually feel alive. It's everyone else I'm hiding from…*with* him. He's once again there for me. I'm not sure I'll ever be able to convey to him how much that means to me.

"Our little secret," he whispers against my lips, like he has direct access to my thoughts.

A secret with Ren.

Wouldn't be the first time.

"Okay, Romeo," I agree, my voice ragged as another orgasm clutches greedily at my body.

My response spurs him on and he fucks me so hard I know I'll be sore tomorrow. I dig my nails into his flesh and hold on for the duration of the ride.

Together we peak with hissed breaths. Wet lips. Tangled souls.

And then together we come back down. Fast and hard. Hurtling toward gravity at breakneck speed.

Reality trickles its way into my brain as his seed trickles its way out of my body. His massive arms slide between my back and the mattress. He then rolls us over onto our sides. I nearly whimper when his fingers brush my hair out of my face. My skin is hot and sticky.

I wish I could see him.

Give a face to the secret.

For now, the dark keeps us hidden.

"What did Duvan want from you?" he questions, his tone sad.

My heart aches in my chest. "For me to be happy. No agendas. No ulterior motives. Nothing in exchange for it. Just to see me smile." Emotion chokes me. "It was that simple."

Ren leans forward and kisses my forehead. "It seems he and I have that in common then," he breathes against me. "I *will* fulfil his wish. We *will* see you smile. You *will* be happy, Juliet."

A smile tugs at my lips from hearing the nickname.

In his pitch-black bedroom, he may not see it, but I sure hope he can feel it.

# IX | Ren

SUNLIGHT POURS IN THROUGH MY WINDOW AND BLANKETS Brie in its warmth. Even the sun wants her. She's the gravity. We all simply orbit around her.

Lifting up on my elbow, I watch her as she sleeps. Her brows aren't pinched together in pain. Her lips aren't drawn into a sad frown. Her brown eyes don't pool with unshed tears.

She's at peace.

Asleep in my bed.

Pride fills my chest. She hasn't run from me. If anything, she's run straight for me. It's where she belongs now that her world has been blown to bits. I won't let anything or anyone touch her again. Her tattered heart belongs to me. I'll mend it until the day I die. I'm still watching her when my phone buzzes from the table. With a groan, I roll over to see who's texting. I see I've missed a few.

**Calder: You do realize there are other people in this house?**

**Calder: I thought you'd be a one-minute man or some shit but that crap went on for hours. WTF dude?**

**Calder: Would have been cooler if she would have accidentally called you Steve…**

**Calder: Oh, Teev! Give it to me! I've got a clue for you right here…**

I roll my eyes at his stupid texts from early this morning.

**Me: You're a dick.**

His response is immediate.

**Calder: A dick that didn't get any sleep because your girl's moans kept me up all night. Oh, Romeo! Oh, Juliet! What is that anyway? Some sort of Shakespearean kink? Must be a thing. I'm googling it.**

I steal a glance at Brie. Last night had been fucking fabulous. And afterward, I held her while she slept. She was more relaxed than the night before. It felt good to give her some relief.

**Calder: Fucking forget it. I can't believe I just googled that shit. Luciana won't stop laughing now.**

He then sends me some Shakespeare porn that has me choking back laughter, so I don't wake up Brie.

**Me: You're a sick fuck.**

I slide out of bed and throw on a pair of jeans before slipping out of the bedroom. Calder and Luciana are nowhere to be found. After I start some coffee, I text him back.

**Me: Where are you?**

**Calder: Denny's. Thought Luci might want to get out of the house.**

*Luci?*

**Me: Thanks for the invite, asshole.**

**Calder: According to my eavesdropping, you ate your**

fill last night.

**Me: I hate you.**

While I wait for him to respond, I stir some sugar into my coffee. Eventually, my punk-ass brother replies.

**Calder: You're going to hate me even more. Mom's on her way. I was supposed to warn you but then I thought it would be funny if she saw you butt-ass naked with Gabe's daughter. Bye, Teev.**

A growl rumbles from me just as the doorbell rings.

Fucking hell.

I don't even make it to the door before it swings open. Mom beams at me. Toto sits on her hip and she has Mason in his carrier in her other hand.

"Teev!" Toto screeches and wiggles herself out of Mom's grip.

I can't help but grin at my little buddy and scoop her up as soon as she makes it over to me. "Hey, Toto. Miss me?"

She hugs my neck and lets out another squeal. "Teev!"

Patting her blonde curls, I arch an eyebrow up at Mom. "You can't just blast in through the door, Mom. I have company."

Mom's mouth drops open and her gaze takes in my appearance. I'm sure my hair has that just-fucked look and I'm not even wearing a shirt, for crying out loud. Her cheeks turn bright red as she wrestles Mason's tiny body out of the car seat. "Well, I didn't know!" she exclaims. "I told your brother I was coming. He said you'd be here."

Toto, now curious about my home, wiggles out of my grip. I set her back on her feet to go on a hunt for my coffee. It's too early to deal with this crap without my liquid caffeine. "Want any coffee?" I call out.

Mom follows me into the kitchen. "Wow…"

Looking over my shoulder, I frown at her. "What?"

"That tattoo. It's…"

"Big?" I quip with a smirk.

She laughs. "That too. It's beautiful, Ren."

I'm just taking my first sip of much needed coffee when I hear Brie screech my name from the other room. I slam down my mug and trot toward the bedroom. When I burst through the door, I'm frozen at what I see.

Toto, a big toothy grin on her face, sitting on Brie's chest and petting her dark brown hair. Brie's eyes are wide and horrified but she makes no move to push Toto away.

"Ahhh, fuck," I hiss.

Mom swats at my back. "Don't cuss around her. She learned the word *shit* the other day from your father and has said it probably a thousand times since." When she pushes past me, she too, pauses. "Oh, dear. You do have company."

*Fucking Calder.*

"Uh, Jesus," I groan and run my fingers through my hair before I stalk over to the bed. "I'm sorry." I scoop Toto's nosy ass up and storm back toward the door. "Mom, take Toto and wait in the living room. Please. Brie and I'll be out in a sec."

Mom's eyes are wide with understanding. She steals another glance at Brie before she ushers Toto out of my room. When I turn to look at Brie, she's chewing on her bottom lip. God, she looks so fuckable this morning with her messy bed hair. She's every man's wet dream with the sheet barely tugged over her generous breasts. If my mother weren't waiting for an explanation in the other room, I'd rip the sheet from Brie's grip and give her something to smile about this morning.

"I'm sorry it had to happen this way," I groan. "If you

want, I can make them leave. You don't have to meet…" I close my eyes and let out a huff. "Your sister."

When I risk a glance at her, she's still frowning. "Technically, I just met her." Her tone is cold but then she seems to soften. "I can do this."

Her simple words mean so much. I love Toto. Who wouldn't love Toto? I want Brie to love her too. Both Toto and Brie could use a sister. Their dad is a little on the special side.

"You're so fucking brave, Brie," I tell her as I stride over to her. I grip her tousled hair and tilt her head back. She lets out a soft moan when I give her a hard kiss. When I finally pull away from her, her eyes flash with anger.

"I haven't brushed my teeth!"

I smirk and shrug my shoulders. "Tasted pretty sweet to me. You don't hear me complaining."

"Who said it was *my* breath I was disgusted about?" she retorts back, her brow lifted up in challenge.

Laughing, I shake my head. "Keep looking at me that way, woman, and I'll give my mother something to be disgusted about when I fuck you so hard you scream loud enough to scare the babies."

She gapes at me. "You wouldn't…"

I slide my leg between her thighs. "Want to test me?" My knee slides up and I nudge her right where I'll put my dirty little mouth if she keeps up the sassy talk.

She's about to respond when Toto starts banging her tiny fists on my door. "Teev! Teev!"

I snap my gaze to Brie and give her a wolfish grin. "We'll continue this discussion later."

The flicker in her previously dull eyes tells me she's looking forward to it.

Awkward doesn't even begin to describe this moment. Brie sits beside me on the couch. Toto is in my lap and keeps petting Brie like she's some sort of exotic animal. And Mom stares at Brie in wonder with Mason suckling on her tit.

Where is Dad or Calder or fucking Gabe?

"Toni is your sister," I tell Brie, my voice soft.

Toto turns and grins at me. "Sissy?" She points at Brie in question.

Brie's hard gaze softens a bit. I know she's uncomfortable around my sister's toddler but these people are her family whether she likes it or not. Toto didn't do anything wrong. If anything, she's the only thing that Hannah and Gabe ever did right.

"Yep," I tell her and tug at a curl. "That's your sissy."

"Why do you call her Toto?" Brie questions.

I can tell Toto wants to crawl into Brie's lap but she hesitates, probably sensing the stress that seems to be rippling from her.

"Your dad calls her that so it kind of stuck."

Toto lets out a needy little whine and regards Brie with the saddest puppy dog eyes I've ever seen. That's a look she learned from her momma. Brie bites on her lip as if she's mentally battling with herself. Finally, though, she reaches for her sister. Toto crawls into her lap and lays her head on her shoulder. Her tiny hands begin playing with Brie's hair.

"Sissy pwetty."

Brie, who was stiff, relaxes and she pats Toto on her back.

"You're pretty too."

I flash Brie a supportive smile before turning to look over at Mom. Tears roll silently down her cheeks. After a moment, she finds her voice. "You look just like your dad," Mom says, her voice quivering.

Brie regards her with a frown. "I look like my mother too. But she was killed."

Mom flinches as if Brie's words were an actual slap to her face. "I'm so sorry, sweetheart. I am so, so sorry."

Brie, who seemed poised for a fight, deflates just as quickly as she'd puffed out. "That was rude. I didn't mean to…" she trails off and jerks her teary gaze to mine.

"Some bad shit happened," I assure her, "and you're not wrong to feel angry or to lash out. If anyone knows how it feels, it's Mom." I smile at Mom and hope she can see how broken Brie is. That she's not being a bitch…she's just hurt.

"My mother died too. And then my father was killed by my high school boyfriend." Mom lowers her gaze. "People hurt me. They stole from me. They took away everything I loved." She sniffles as she burps Mason. "Your father was one of those people."

Brie snaps her gaze to my mother. "What?"

"They told me what that man did to you in Colombia. And then what happened to your husband," Mom says. "I'm so sorry, honey. I just want you to know that if you ever need someone to talk to, I'm here. I know how it feels to be raped and held against your will. I know how it feels to be a captive. I know how it feels to watch the ones you love bleed out in front of you." She dabs at her cheek with Mason's bib. "And I also know how awful it feels to have to have contact with those who hurt you. The hardest thing I ever had to do was accept your sister. My rapist's child."

Brie starts to cry. "But he's my daddy." Even though she argues with my mom, I can sense she believes every word. "He wouldn't do that, right?"

Mom swallows and her lips purse into a firm line. "He did. It was a long time ago but he did."

I attempt to comfort Brie by pulling her closer but she's still on her quest to understand and shakes me away.

"I don't know if I can accept this—what you're saying," she chokes out, her voice breathless. Her eyes flit over to her little sister and she frowns. "Any of this."

"I can't imagine how it would feel to have to accept your mother's murderer's child," Mom murmurs. "I know that it hurts. That it is confusing. That it makes you angry."

"Mom-mom," Toto says sadly as she climbs off Brie's lap and runs over to Mom. "Don't cwy."

Mom pulls her into her side and kisses her blonde head. "But some of us just have to be stronger because the rest of the world simply is not."

Brie buries her face into my side as a loud sob escapes her. I hold her to me as she cries. My poor, broken, beautiful girl.

"Daddy always told me that people would say he did bad things. I just never understood what those things were. He certainly never explained them." Brie lets out a painful cry but sits up to look at my mother. "He might have hurt you, and for that I'm sorry, but he was the best father anyone could have asked for."

Mom nods and smiles at her. "I don't doubt that for a minute, sweetheart. I've seen how he behaves around Toto. Gabe isn't all bad. For ten years of my life, he was my entire world. I'm not trying to turn you against him. I'm simply telling you I understand how you feel."

Brie's hand finds mine and she squeezes it as if she requires my strength. "I still love him."

"I know." Mom winks at her.

Something passes between them. Something powerful. Something solid.

"Umm, Mrs. McPherson…"

"Baylee," Mom corrects.

Brie swipes away her tears with the back of her hand and begins resurrecting the wall that protects her. "Can I get the name of your obstetrician? I'm not sure who to go to and I'm going to need to get some prenatal tests done soon."

Mom's eyes drop to Brie's stomach and then flicker to mine. I give her a slight shake of my head. *I'm not the father.* Understanding flashes in them. Not relief, though. Sadness. "Of course, Brie. I've got a card in my bag. In another month or two, Mason will be too big for his bassinet. I could loan it to you if you'd like."

"I would like that," Brie assures her. "And, Baylee?"

"Yes, honey?"

"I'm sorry he hurt you. I wouldn't wish that on anyone."

Mom smiles at her. "What doesn't kill us makes us stronger. They may try to tear our hearts apart…" She strokes at Toto's hair and looks fondly at her. "But they don't understand, our hearts are made of steel. Women like us are unbreakable. Even when we're shattered into a thousand bits. We just find a way to gather up what's left, walk into the fire otherwise known as life, and weld our most precious piece back together again." Mom kisses Mason's forehead before leveling her gaze at Brie. "This is life, baby. And you're going to conquer it."

# X | Brie

I FIDGET ON THE EXAM TABLE AS I WAIT FOR THE DOCTOR to see me. The nurse had me pee in a cup and drew some blood after having me fill out a mountain of paperwork. Baylee had offered to come with me, but I'm glad that it's Ren who's here with me.

His shoulders are tense as he stares out the window. It's been a week since I met my sister and his mother. A whole week of us being intimate at night but friends during the day. Something about the daylight makes me feel exposed. Like I've done something wrong. Like I've betrayed Duvan by letting Ren put me back together again.

The daylight instills guilt.

Which is why I keep him at arm's length.

Until his bedroom door closes at night.

When he draws me into his arms and kisses away all the pain. I count down the minutes until we're alone in the dark. It's the only time I feel somewhat normal. I'd thought he'd be upset with me. That my standoffishness during the day would hurt his feelings.

But Ren is strong.

It's as if he has direct access into my head. I don't have to tell him because he gets it. Ren respects my boundaries and doesn't breach them.

I hate what I'm doing to him but it helps me. I'm selfish because I need him to be two different people for me at two different times.

"Are you nervous?" he questions, his steely blues darting to mine.

I stop chewing on my fingernail and nod. "I am. What if I'm not really pregnant? What if I don't have his baby inside me? It's all I have left of him…" The stupid emotions overwhelm me once again. Tears streak down my cheeks. But before they can even drip from my jaw, Ren is out of his seat and standing beside the exam table pulling me into his arms.

"You're sick every morning, Brie. Your tits are huge. And you haven't had a period in a while, right? You're pregnant. Stop worrying. His baby is safe," he assures me.

I let my best friend hug me tight. We may not carry on a sexual relationship when the sun can stare at me with disdain in its eyes, but we still touch. His hugs are soothing to me. They're needed and always come at the right time.

Luciana and I are tight, but she can't give this to me.

Vee, at one time could have, but she's nowhere to be found.

The thought of Vee has my heart aching. I don't know where she went. Ren's father is looking into tracking her whereabouts. According to his records, her apartment and parents' house are still being paid for. It's as if she and her mom left on a vacation or something. Knowing her stupid mom, she probably took Vee to some resort so they could deal with the stress of losing Heath by getting pedicures and massages and sipping mimosas.

I'd ask Oscar but he's unreachable. He won't answer his phone or his emails. The last I'd heard about him was from Rafe. But I can't get in touch with Rafe now either. Everything is all so weird.

The door clicks open and someone walks in. Ren kisses the top of my head before releasing me to go sit back down. An Asian woman with black hair and a pretty smile walks in wearing a lab coat.

"Hello, Mrs. Rojas. I'm Dr. Ling," the woman greets and extends her small hand.

I shake it and force a smile. "Hi."

She sits down on a stool and opens the laptop on the counter. Quickly, she scans through the information. "Well, you're definitely pregnant according to your bloodwork and urine sample. Congratulations," she says with a grin. "And based on when you said your last period was, that puts you at twelve weeks."

My heart races in my chest.

This is real.

I'm pregnant with Duvan's baby.

I will carry on a piece of him.

"Would you like to see your baby?" she questions. "At this stage, we should be able to get a pretty good picture for you."

My gaze jerks over to Ren and he's beaming. He nods his head before rising and striding back over to me. He takes my hand. "Brie, this is exciting."

Tears well in my eyes, and I nod at the doctor. "Yes. Please."

109

She calls in a nurse and they begin prepping me for a vaginal ultrasound. My hand squeezes Ren's strong one as anxiety spikes through me. The only thing keeping me sane through this entire ordeal is the breathtaking smile on his handsome face.

He's happy for me.

That thought elates me.

"This will feel a little uncomfortable, but just try to relax," Dr. Ling says in a calm voice. I feel pressure as she pushes the lubricated wand into me. The nurse turns some dials on the screen beside the bed.

"You're doing a great job," Ren whispers before kissing me on the forehead.

I smile back at him.

"You two are a cute couple," the young nurse says with a grin. "How long have you been married?"

My heart stops beating in my chest. Her simple question reminds me of the fact that my child will never have a father. That we'll have to deal with these questions until the day we die.

"What's that?" Ren interjects, pointing at the screen. I'm thankful for the distraction and the fact that he reads me so well.

The nurse turns her attention to the screen. Her smile falls immediately. "Umm, Dr. Ling?"

Dr. Ling's eyebrows furrow together as she concentrates. "Yes," she murmurs. "I see that. Let me make sure first."

Ren's gaze snaps to mine and terror flickers in his eyes. I don't like the look because it scares me. Everything about the way they're acting is scaring me.

"Volume, Nurse Ellie," Dr. Ling instructs.

A moment later, a loud thumping fills the room. All fear drains away from me as I focus on the beautiful sound.

"That is your baby's heartbeat," Dr. Ling says. She moves the wand around inside of me. A moment later, I hear another sound. The cadence slightly different. "And this is your other baby's heartbeat."

Time stands still as I process her words. Nurse Ellie is beaming at me pointing to two different grainy blobs on the screen.

"T-Two?" I stutter out.

Ren bends over and boldly kisses me on the mouth. "Two babies," he breathes against my lips. "Congratulations, Momma."

Tears roll out of my eyes and Ren swipes them away with his thumbs. His eyes twinkle with delight and it fills me with warmth. Two babies. This is better than good. This is perfect. Of course Duvan would knock me up with a litter of little tiger cubs. Of course he would.

"I'm speechless," I manage to choke out.

Dr. Ling chuckles. "Most parents are when they find out they're having twins. Come back in another month for your sixteen-week checkup and we may be able to determine the sex of the babies."

Ren gives me a lopsided grin that makes my heart flop in my chest. Nurse Ellie pulls some photographs from the printer and then hands a stack to me. When she hands Ren a picture, she beams at him. "Congratulations to you too, Daddy. You did good work." She gives him a wink.

I don't have the heart to tell her he isn't the father. Thankfully, Ren doesn't confirm nor deny her words. He simply takes the picture and stares proudly at it. My heart is too small and shredded to handle all of this happiness at once. I'm overwhelmed.

"I'm going to set you up with some prenatal vitamins, but other than that, keep doing what you're doing. Your weight is a healthy amount and the babies look great," Dr. Ling tells me as she stands.

*Babies.*

I'm having two.

The moment we exit the building and the late October breeze whips around us, Ren scoops me into his arms. I let out a laugh when he spins me in a circle before putting me back on my feet.

His hair is styled in a messy way that looks good on him. The stubble on his cheeks has gotten thicker and I love the way it feels when his mouth kisses me in the dark all over my most sensitive places. Steely blue eyes shine with pride and love and excitement. I don't think he's ever looked as sexy as he does now.

"Brie," he says, his tone low. His smile falls and he regards me with a severe look. "You keep looking at me that way, and I won't be able to control what happens next." His head lifts up to the sky, making his Adam's apple bulge from his throat. "In case you didn't notice, it's broad daylight." He draws his chin back down and glares at me with a wicked gleam in his eyes. "The things I want to do to you are too sinful for this time of day."

His words cause my panties to dampen. The rules and

boundaries I have in place with Ren are slightly skewed and greyed out right now. For once I'd like to watch the way his full lips suck on my inner thigh until it leaves a mark. For once, I'd like to see the way his cock stretches me open as he slowly slides into me. For once I'd like to stare into his blues as he drives into me. Thoughts of sex with Ren aren't helping my situation. Like always, he reads me so well. Hunger flashes in his gaze.

"God," he growls. "You're so fucking sexy. I know it isn't what you want to hear right now but I can't not say it." His fingers spear into my hair and he tugs until I'm looking up at him. The parking lot is full of people but he doesn't care. His mouth once again descends upon mine like when he so boldly kissed me in the exam room. This time, though, his intent is darker—like our nights. I let out a moan the second his lips press against mine. A starved growl rumbles from him as he deepens our kiss.

I clutch his shirt to hold him in place. Truth is, I don't want the kiss to ever end. In the daylight, the kiss warms me. It's freeing. People can see. We can see. Our teeth clash together as we kiss, as though there might not be another chance. Having lost Duvan has shown me that you never know what the future holds so you have to take those chances when they're presented to you.

He finally breaks our kiss when we're both panting for air and slides his palms to the sides of my neck. His forehead leans against mine as he grins at me.

"Oh, Romeo," I say with a chuckle. I can't help but think that several months ago, when I was still locked away in my tower, I'd have gone wild over a kiss like that. Very romantic. Very Romeo. Very Ren.

"Speaking of, Juliet, do you want to go to the costume store? Calder's having a Halloween party tomorrow night. He's been inviting a shit-ton of people. It could be fun," he says, waggling his eyebrows at me.

My heart sinks.

Ren probably wants us to dress up as Romeo and Juliet.

"I want to be a tigress," I blurt out.

His dark brown eyebrow lifts up in amusement, not disappointment like I would have thought. "I wouldn't expect anything less." He gives my ass a squeeze. "Now get in the truck before I turn into a beast and maul you."

The visual has me stalling for just a moment.

I like it when Ren goes into beast mode.

"There," I tell him, pointing at a townhouse at the end of his street. "Let's go look."

He pulls his truck into the driveway. This townhouse is two-story and stucco and has a direct view of the ocean. I like that it's close to Ren. As much as I've enjoyed sleeping in his bed each night, I need to think of giving my babies a real home.

A multicolored strand of flags flaps in the wind. A sign boasting Open House hangs above the garage. I've not even been inside yet and I already feel drawn to this place. We climb out and Ren takes my hand. His grip makes me feel secure. Together, we enter the place. Before we even make it through the front door, a man in a black suit with a blinding white smile greets us. As soon as he quickly assesses us, his smile falters. I'm sure he was hoping for someone older.

"What can I help you kids with?" he questions, irritation bubbling in his voice.

Ren bristles at his tone. "Well," Ren bites out, dropping his gaze to the realtor's nametag, "Conrad, you can start by giving us a tour. Unless you're too busy for that. We can certainly show ourselves around."

Conrad opens his mouth to reply when another couple walks in the front door. He sizes the older couple up and makes a quick decision. "Please," he says, "feel free to show yourselves around."

Ren tenses but I tug him away from the asshole. "I'd rather take the tour with you instead. He's a douchebag," I mutter.

He chuckles and lets me guide him down the hallway. Everything is perfect. Brand new hardwood floors. Granite countertops in the kitchen. Fancy stainless steel appliances and fixtures. Once I'm satisfied I've properly looked at everything downstairs, I let Ren guide me up the stairs of the fully furnished home.

"Do you think they'll sell the furniture too?" I ponder aloud.

He stops at the top of the steps and frowns at me. "You really want to buy it?"

I swallow and nod. "I want to give my babies a home."

His gaze bores into mine for a long moment. "Okay, then. Let's check out the rest, Momma." That's twice now he's called me Momma and both times, it's filled me with warmth.

We carefully inspect each bedroom. There are two smaller bedrooms and a larger master. So Luciana will have a place to stay too. I'll probably put the twins together. This house is perfect.

Ren drags me into the master bathroom. He grins when I shriek over the size of the jet bathtub and walk-in shower.

"I'm going to buy it," I tell him proudly.

He walks over to the bathroom door and locks it. Then, he saunters over to me. "It's perfect. Just like you." I let out a whimper when he grabs my hips and turns me to face the mirror.

Compared to Ren, I look like a shrimp. My dark brown hair is messy and windblown, but the look on my face isn't one I've seen in a while. Happiness. Hope. Pride. I'm smiling, and it looks good on me. He, of course, looks like perfection in a tight white T-shirt that showcases every single one of his muscles. His large hands seem to swallow my waist as he rests them on my hips.

The lines have become blurry with him.

I want him in this moment.

Not tonight after the lights have gone out.

Now.

As if back inside my head, he reaches for the light switch. I shake my head at our reflection. "Leave them on."

He gives me a clipped nod before he sweeps my hair away from my neck. His lips are soft on my flesh as he places hot kisses there. One of his massive hands slides to my front and grips my breast through a Nirvana shirt of his I stole.

"Are you sure you want to see this?" he murmurs and then his teeth tug at my flesh near my ear. "I'm going to fuck you right now against this counter. In this house. For those assholes downstairs to hear. Can you handle seeing it happen? Last chance for me to turn off the lights, baby."

My eyes flutter closed at his bold words. I'm wet and needy for him. Screw my boundaries. I want to see this.

Grabbing on to his hand, I guide him lower until his fingers graze against my clit through my yoga pants. Pleasure jolts through me at the simple touch.

"I want to see," I whisper, my unsure eyes meeting his. "I need to see."

He grabs the bottom of my shirt and pulls it hastily from my body. The bra I'm wearing is way too small now and my tits are spilling out of the top of it. His hands cup them in a reverent way for a moment before he dances his fingers along to my back to unlatch my bra. When it falls to the floor and my heavy breasts are freed, our eyes once again meet in the mirror.

"You're so goddamned beautiful, Brie. I'll never get tired of looking at you," he growls. His tongue finds my neck and he laps at me. "I'll never get tired of tasting you." Then, he sinks his teeth into my skin in a playful way. "I'll never get tired of biting you." He roughly hooks his thumbs into the top of my pants and shoves them down. With one of his large hands, he pushes the middle of my back until my palms are on the countertop and my face is inches from the glass. His hands grope my ass cheeks for a second before he runs a long fingertip between my thighs. He finds my wet opening and breaches it with his finger. I let out a needy moan and wiggle my hips at him.

"Ren…"

He does that sexy man thing where he reaches behind his neck and yanks his shirt up over his head in a way that looks sinful. I watch him jerk at his belt and then his jeans slide to the floor. His impressive cock is freed and slides along the crack of my ass, causing me to shiver with anticipation. He fists his erection and guides it into my wet opening, drawing a whine from me. When he's pushed in to the hilt, he flashes me a wicked grin that has me clenching around him.

Seeing this makes it better.

Reality isn't always a bitch.

The darkness isn't always preferable to the light.

"I'll never get tired of fucking you, baby."

He slides all the way out before slamming into me again. I cry out and grip the countertop. When my eyes close as I give in to the pleasure, pain at my skull forces them back open. Ren's blue eyes glimmer wildly and he has my hair tangled in his grip.

"Eyes open," he growls as his hips piston into me.

My mouth is parted open and my eyes are hooded. Swollen breasts bounce in front of me with every thrust he delivers.

This is hot.

We're hot.

"Oh, God..." I whimper, my legs beginning to shake with impending pleasure.

His rough palm slides around my hip to my front where he captures my clit between his thumb and finger. The hand that's gripping my hair pulls me toward him so his chest is up against my back. He can't thrust with me standing upright so he focuses on massaging my clit. My eyes start to close again, so he tugs my hair hard enough to remind me of his command. I bite down on my lip and meet his gaze head on. The fire that blazes in his blues consumes me. I give in to the expert way he touches me and cry out as my entire body convulses. The moment my legs begin to wobble, he pushes me back down onto the counter. Slam after beautiful slam, he thunders into me until he grunts signifying his own release. His heat gushes into me without warning. He slows, and when his cock stops throbbing, he flashes me a crooked, mischievous grin.

"You."

I raise an eyebrow. "Me?"

"Yep. You." Chuckling, he pulls out of me and his seed runs down my inner thigh. Uncaring that we're in a house that doesn't belong to us, he yanks a hand towel off the rack and sets to cleaning me up. We're just pulling on the last of our clothes when someone beats on the door.

Ren smirks at me before sauntering over to the door, his T-shirt still in hand. When he slings it open, Conrad glares at us.

"You need to leave," he snaps.

The couple behind him gapes at us. The woman's neck turns bright red when she sees Ren with no shirt on. It's obvious what we've been up to.

"No," I tell him. "How much?"

Conrad frowns. "I'm sorry but Mr. and Mrs. Sanchez here are putting in an offer. We're about to work up the paperwork as soon as you leave."

Ren lets out a menacing growl, and I flash him a smile letting him know I've got this.

"Conrad. How much are they offering?" I ask again, my voice calm.

He lifts his chin in a snotty way. "Six hundred."

Turning to the couple, I smile. "Is that as high as you can go?"

Mr. Sanchez puffs out his chest. "We have room to negotiate if you're insinuating a bidding war. I assure you, we'll outbid you. We want this townhouse."

I laugh and shake my head. "You may want this town-house, but I *need* this townhouse. I have two little cubs on the way, am obsessed with the beach, and my best friend lives on this street. I also have more money than I know what to do with. So, make your best offer so I can outbid you and we can all move along with our day." Turning toward Conrad, I give him a shrug of my shoulders. "Did I mention I can pay cash?"

Four hours later and a seven hundred grand wire trans-fer, I'm the proud owner of my first home.

# XI | Ren

"**I** CAN'T BELIEVE I BOUGHT A HOUSE," BRIE MURMURS TO herself in the dark.

I'm glad she wanted to spend one more night at my house before moving in to hers. I am selfish and like her in my bed. Having her down the street will be nice, but I don't know where that leaves us.

"Conrad sure changed his tune. Ran that poor couple right out of the house once he realized you were serious." I chuckle just thinking about the greedy sleezeball. My palm finds her bare breast under the sheet and I give her nipple a little pinch. "It was nice getting to see you while we fucked."

She stiffens, but I don't regret my words. It *was* nice. I won't forget the look on her face when I made her come. All stress and worry and sadness was gone as she succumbed to the bliss. *I* made her feel good.

"Ren." A pause. "I'm sorry."

I chuckle and playfully bite her tit. "You weren't sorry when you were coming all over my dick."

She pulls away and then light from the bedside lamp floods the room. When she looks at me, her gaze is sad. "I don't want to use you. I just…" she trails off. "I don't understand how to feel or what to do right now. I'm doing it all wrong, I know. But…"

"It feels so fucking right?"

Her eyes snap to mine and she nods. I grin at her and press soft kisses to her breast that's closest to me. My palm splays out over her stomach that's not as tight as I remember. I'm looking forward to watching it swell. When I look back up at her, a storm brews in her eyes.

"What?" My palm stills on her stomach. "Am I hurting you?"

Her nostrils flare and she shakes her head. "No. You're just…"

"Perfect? Sexy? Amazing?" I tease and nip at her flesh.

She lets out a gasp. "You're just…"

"I could go all night. Funny? Have a beautiful cock? Smart? Hot as fuck?"

A giggle escapes her and it makes my heart rate speed up. "Thank you."

"For being all of the above?" I quirk up a playful eyebrow.

She nods. "Thanks for always being here for me. Through all of my storms, you've been there. Steadying me. Holding me. Assuring me everything would be okay. I feel thankful is all."

I slide back up the bed so I can kiss her. She lets me pull her into my arms and seems just as eager for my mouth. Her fingers thread into my hair as I kiss her deep enough to steal her breath. After a hot, wet kiss, I pull away to look at her. Her plump lips are swollen and red from my facial hair. I love making her flesh turn crimson.

"Am I a bad person?" she questions, tears welling in her chocolate eyes.

I shake my head as I push her onto her back. She parts her legs willingly and lets me slide inside of her. Her breath hitches. I cup her cheek and stare into her glimmering orbs. Neither of us moves, we just remain connected—both physically and emotionally.

"You're one of the best people I know," I tell her firmly. "You've always been strong and resilient. Like a dandelion in a hurricane. The wind rips away parts of you, but you're still left standing after the storm. Sure, you're weathered and changed, but you're still there."

She laughs. "This is me, baby. A hairless dandelion."

I smirk at her and then steal her smile with a kiss. "You're a smartass too."

"Are you going to just sit there with your dick inside me or are you going to fuck me?" she sasses.

I let a growl escape as I snatch both her wrists and press them into the bed. She squirms as she waits for me to fuck her. I'll tease her a bit first. Locking eyes with her, I slowly thrust into her in a teasing manner. Then, I drag my gaze down to watch how my thick cock stretches her with each slide inside her body. My dick is coated with her wetness, which is a total turn on. Lately, in the dark, we've missed some of the small details that mean so much.

Seeing her arousal on my cock is most definitely a detail I never want to miss again.

"Faster, Ren," she grumbles. Very much a growly tigress.

I shake my head and continue teasing her in a torturous way. She resists at first but then begins to learn this rhythm.

Her body quakes and trembles as it anticipates each of my movements.

"You're so fucking wet, baby," I murmur.

She bites on her bottom lip and desire flickers in her eyes.

"I want you to come just like this. Think you can orgasm without me touching your needy clit?" I question, my voice husky.

Panic flashes in her eyes. "I don't know. I want to come so badly."

"You're going to come that way," I tell her in a matter-of-fact tone. "In fact, I have an idea to help make that happen."

She lets out a squeal when I roll us over to where I'm on my back. I release her wrists while she settles herself over my hips. A gasp rushes from her when my cock hits her in the right spot.

"Do more of that," I instruct as I slide my finger along the place where my cock is pushed into her opening, now dripping with arousal. She gasps when I slip it inside along with my dick. I make sure to coat it well before pulling it back out. "Twist around so I can see your sexy ass."

Her eyes widen with fear, but when I grin at her she obeys. Once she's settled with her round ass facing me, I grab her hip to urge her to move. She begins rocking her body and rolling her hips. It feels so fucking good but this is about her. I want her to come without any clitoral stimulation.

"Relax a minute, Brie," I murmur as I tease the tight hole of her ass with my wet finger.

"Ren…"

"Shhh," I urge.

Her dark hair hangs down her back as she looks up at the ceiling. I notice the moment her rigid body seems to relax.

Slowly, I push my thick finger into her tight ass.

"Ohhhh…." she moans.

God, she's so fucking tight.

"That's it, beautiful. Now ride that cock. Make it feel good. I want your hands all over those perfect fucking tits. That clit is off limits, understand? If you're a good girl and come like this, I'll suck on it until you see stars."

She lets out another sound of bliss and begins riding both my dick and my finger. Her ass clenches with each movement. I want to come so fucking badly but I don't dare do it until she's screaming my name.

"You're doing such a good job," I praise. "I love seeing your body. Fuck this bullshit darkness. I only ever want to see you in the light from here on out. Got it, baby?"

She nods and quickens her pace. Her breaths come out quick and ragged with each passing second. "Oh God!" Her body clenches around me for a second before she lets out a roar. A motherfucking roar. Like a woman possessed, she shudders wildly as pleasure takes over. It steals her away from me for a moment, and I allow her the brief, torrid affair with bliss because I know she'll be back with me soon. As she crashes back to reality, I release my own climax into her. I'll never grow tired of fucking this beautiful, broken woman.

When we both still, I slip my finger slowly out of her body. Then, she eases herself off my cock. Before she gets too far away, I give her sexy ass a *thwap*.

"Hey!" she screeches and scrambles away from me. Her smile is so fucking pretty.

"You liked it," I tell her smugly as I sit up on my elbows. "Seems like you're into a lot of kinky shit these days. I'd be an asshole if I didn't deliver what you secretly want."

She arches a brow at me. "Who says it's a secret?"

"So it's public knowledge that you want my cock in your ass?" I retort back.

"Ren!" she scoffs. Heat colors her chest and throat.

"I guess you *do* still have some secrets," I tell her with a big-ass grin. "I won't tell anyone. But you'll have to be quiet when I'm fucking that pretty little ass because they're going to hear you otherwise. You're the loud one, not me."

"Oh my God," she grumbles. Despite her tone, her smile gives her away. "You're impossible." She bounces off toward the bathroom, her butt jiggling at me as if to fucking tease me.

I scramble off the bed, trailing after her. "Don't deny it, baby. The heart wants what the heart wants."

My words—meant to tease—seem to strike a chord with her because her smile falls in the bathroom mirror. Her eyes well with tears and she drops her gaze to the sink. Coming up behind her, I wrap my arms around her and bury my nose in her hair.

"Don't feel guilty for being happy, Gabriella Rojas," I murmur to her. "He would have hated that."

Her eyes snap back up to mine, understanding flashing in them. She doesn't have to say a word. I've always been able to read my girl.

And she's always been my girl...even when she wasn't.

I slide both palms to her stomach and smile at her. "Are you happy?"

Her smile is shy and she nods. "I am."

"Good," I tell her firmly. "Harness that feeling and don't ever fucking let it go. You deserve it, baby. You've always deserved it."

"You're seriously not wearing that," Calder says, barely holding in a chuckle.

I look down at my carefully put together costume and shrug before I start bouncing my tennis ball at the wall again. "What's wrong with it?"

"You look like a douchebag. An 80s one at that." He shakes his head as if he's embarrassed of me.

"And your costume is any better? What the hell are you supposed to be, anyway?" I question as I toss the tennis ball at him.

He catches it and flashes me a wicked Calder grin. "A puppeteer."

"Like Geppetto?"

The ball gets launched back at me. "You'll see." He whistles and soon my bedroom door opens. Luciana waltzes in wearing a grin that matches his. Those two are up to something. Two partners in a crime I haven't figured out just yet. If Brie were here, she'd be calling her friend out right about now, demanding to know what's going on. But she wanted to get ready at her house. I'm supposed to pick her up in half an hour.

"Luci," Calder says, and beckons for her to come to him. Her makeup has been done up artfully so that she looks kind of like a doll. Dark hair pulled into pigtails. Rosy red cheeks. Two black lines drawn down her chin from each corner of her mouth to her jaw. I put it together and I'm already shaking my head.

"Don't you think this is a little insensitive," I mutter through clenched teeth.

Calder stiffens as if the thought just now occurred to him. He snaps his wide-eyed gaze to Luciana. "I thought it would be funny—" He runs his fingers through his hair in frustration. "Not insulting. Jesus! Am I insulting you, Luci?"

She shakes her head in vehemence and steps closer to him. Her brown eyes sparkle with delight. He raises his palm to her cheek for a brief moment as if he's caught up in her gaze. But then, as if cold water has been splashed on him, he jerks his hand away. Disappointment mars her pretty features for just a moment before she forces it away with a smile.

Calder clears his throat before sliding his hand up under the back of her shirt. Her white T-shirt tightens around her breasts and her midriff shows.

"Hey Teev," Calder chirps in a cheesy girl voice through clenched teeth. "The 80s called, they want that abomination you call an outfit back." As he speaks, Luciana animatedly moves her mouth as if the words are coming from her.

"A ventriloquist and a dummy," I grumble. "Unbelievable."

Calder once again talks in his stupid voice as Luciana acts out, as if she's speaking. "I only see one dummy here and I'm staring right at him." Luciana leans forward and waggles her eyebrows at me. I can't help but laugh because they are so damn stupid.

"Go away," I groan. "Don't you have some Martha Stewart shit in the oven for your lame Halloween party?"

"Fuuuuck," Calder grumbles and runs out of the room.

Luciana starts giggling, and I flip her off. "Laugh it up." But then I grow serious and sit up on my bed. "You two seem fast friends," I probe.

The blush that creeps up her neck immediately gives her away. She pulls her phone out of her pocket and starts tapping away like mad before handing it to me.

*He's not into me or anything. Not like you're thinking. He just likes me as friend.*

I lift an eyebrow up. "I've known Calder for nearly two decades. That's more than just friendship."

Hope flashes in her eyes as she steals her phone back. She taps out a response.

*The Beebs is not into me. He can't even kiss me. I have no tongue, remember?*

Tears well in her eyes and she looks down at her feet. I grab her wrist and pull her to sit down beside me. Wrapping an arm around her, I hug her to me.

"Luciana," I tell her firmly, "you can kiss without tongue."

She types on her phone and holds it up for me.

*I've never been kissed at all. I'm afraid I'll disgust anyone who tries…*

At this I laugh. "Calder is pretty fucking disgusting. He'd be lucky to get to kiss you."

She giggles and it's like little bells ringing on Christmas day.

"Now tell me about this Beebs nickname," I urge and flash her a grin.

She bites on her bottom lip and her neck turns bright red again. Finally, she lets out a resigned sigh and taps out a message.

*He looks like Justin Bieber. Soooo hot. Don't tell him I said that!*

I start laughing so hard tears roll down my cheeks. She slaps me and then flips me off. I'm still rolling when Calder comes sauntering back in. His gaze snaps between Luciana and me sitting next to each other on the bed. Then, he stalks over to her. "Is he making fun of you?" he demands as he hauls her to her feet and into his protective arms.

"N-No," I laugh. "I'm making fun of *you*, dumbass."

She shoots me a warning glare, and I wink at her. "Don't worry," I assure her, "your secret is safe with me."

Calder growls at me before escorting her out of my room. My stomach hurts from laughing so hard. The Beebs. I guess he sort of looks like him. They both have stupid tattoos. But does Justin Bieber know how to make pigs-in-a-blanket and put on a party that Martha Stewart would be proud of? I think not.

I'm just getting ready to go pick up Brie when my phone rings.

Without looking at the caller ID, I answer it.

"Yeah?"

"Let me talk to my daughter."

Gabe.

Rolling my eyes, I start gathering what I need before I leave the house. "She's not here. What do you want?"

He lets out a frustrated sigh. "Rafe called me. He's a friend of Duvan's. Was there with us when she made that deal with Diego." He growls and anger ripples from him. "I'm going to fuck him up one day."

I scowl. "Who the hell is Diego?"

"An asshole who's going to get what's coming to him. I still don't know what he said or did to Brie, but she was pretty shaken up after we left. If I find out he touched her—"

Red blurs my vision and my hand fists. I'm seconds from sending it through the sheetrock. "She didn't say anything about this Diego shit. What would she make a deal with him about?"

He grumbles. "Sold the crack factory."

I don't correct him even though it was coke.

"Made a cool twelve mil for it too," he continues, pride in his voice. "My baby is a master negotiator."

And rich, I think.

I'd assumed Gabe gave her money or that she'd had some leftover from when she'd sold the house. I didn't know she sold the coke plant too. And to a cartel king, no less.

"Why did Rafe call?"

"He said trouble is on the horizon. He thinks Diego might be in cahoots with that Esteban fuck. Another bastard I'm going to murder. I wanted her to be on the lookout. The last thing we need is some drug trafficker hurting my daughter. It happened once before but it won't happen again," he snarls.

"Right. I'll keep a close watch on her." I'm already gathering my shit and walking out the door after her.

"Ren," he grunts. "I'm coming to your party tonight. Your dad told me about it. If I were some criminal cocksucker, a costume party would be the perfect place to find someone. I'll stay out of sight but I'm going to be there in case any shady shit goes down."

I roll my eyes. Ever since Toto came onto the scene, Dad and Gabe act like they're best fucking pals. I don't even know how Mom puts up with that crap.

"Whatever," I mutter. "Just don't upset her. She's happy, man. Let's keep her that way."

He lets out a resigned sigh. "She'll be happier when I serve her Esteban's dead cock on a platter."

# XII
## Brie

I STARE INTO THE SAME BATHROOM MIRROR REN FUCKED me in front of and frown. The outfit I'd bought at the Halloween store yesterday doesn't look as cute on today. Perhaps spandex was not a good idea for a pregnant-with-twins woman to be wearing. At least if I'd gone with Juliet, I'd be wearing a big, flowy dress.

Grumbling, I paint on whiskers and a black nose. My hair has been pulled back into a sleek ponytail and I've put on a headband with tiger ears on it. The tiger striped cat suit I'm wearing fits like a glove. But when I turn to the side, I can see my belly protrude. It doesn't look like a pregnancy swell…it just looks like I ate too many tacos at lunch.

I did eat too many tacos at lunch thanks to Calder. Between him and Luciana in the kitchen, they cooked us up one helluva lunch.

I let out a huff of frustration. Too late to change my outfit now. I'm just attaching my tail and slipping into some black flats when I hear music. I step out of my bathroom and walk over to my bedroom window, which overlooks the driveway. As I near it, I recognize the music.

"In Your Eyes" by Peter Gabriel blasts from outside.

A smile tugs at my lips.

Ren gets me.

He always has.

With a cheesy grin on my face, I run over to the window and draw back the curtains. Sure enough, Ren stands in my driveway in front of his black truck. The music booms from his truck but he's holding up a handmade cardboard boom box. His dark hair has been styled into a geeky 80s style to match that of John Cusack's from the *Say Anything* movie. He's nailed the costume. But unlike nerdy John, Ren looks hotter than hell in his 80s movie getup. The white Clash T-shirt fits him like it was painted on. He wears a tan trench coat over it with the sleeves pushed up to his elbows. But the pants and shoes are what have me giggling. His grey pants have red stripes going down the sides and are tapered at the bottom. The white high-top sneakers have to have been stolen from an old man's closet somewhere because I know they don't make shoes like that anymore.

Lifting the window, I lean out and laugh. "Lloyd!"

He fist pumps the air because he knows I get his silly costume. "Get your sexy ass down here, little tigress. I've been dying to see your tight body in spandex ever since you bought that damn outfit."

Not exactly what Lloyd said in the movie…but it's definitely better.

I've long forgotten about my insecurities as I close the window to head downstairs. By the time I sling open the front door, he's abandoned his cardboard box and is waiting on the porch with his hands shoved in his pockets. Even though he tried to dork himself out, he's still so good looking.

Strong, chiseled jaw.

Piercing steel blue eyes.

Sexy stubble sprinkled on his handsome face.

Rushing over to him, I throw my arms around his neck and hug him. "You're such a nerd," I say with a chuckle.

His powerful arms squeeze me to him and he inhales my hair. "Good thing you're a nerd too. A sexy nerd but still a total nerd. You're the one who likes these goofy movies, not me."

I pull away and regard him with a lifted brow. "Is that right? How many times did you watch *Say Anything* to get this costume perfect?"

He grins at me sheepishly. "Yeah, yeah. Get your pretty butt in the car."

When I pull away, he gives my ass a slap. I narrow my eyes at him and make a growling sound. He grabs me by the tail and pulls me back into his arms. His hot mouth breathes against my neck near my ear as his palms roam my spandexed front, settling on my tits.

"You're hot as fuck, kitty."

I laugh. "Kitty? Have you seen the claw marks I left on you last night? I am tigress. Hear me roar."

He pinches my nipple through the spandex. "Okay, tigress," he concedes. "And for the record, I like your claw marks on me. Gotta love a woman who marks her territory."

*Territory.* Is he mine?

My heart rate quickens in my chest.

He is.

I don't let guilt steal away our moment. Instead, I close

my eyes and relax in his arms. He peppers kisses along the outside of my neck. Then, he twists me back around so we're facing one another. His strong fingers grip my jaw in a gentle way.

"You're so beautiful, Brie." His brows are furrowed as he makes this proclamation.

I stare deep into his intense blue eyes. "So are you, Ren."

We hold each other's stares for a long moment. Then, he dips down and brushes a soft kiss on my lips. It's only a tease and I crave more. A car door slams loudly from nearby and it makes him tense. He starts to tug me to the truck.

"We're too exposed out here," he mutters, a slight bite to his voice.

I jolt at the sudden change in his demeanor. "No more darkness," I remind him.

He shuts me in the truck and then soon joins me. The keys sit in the ignition but he makes no move to turn the engine over. When he turns his head toward mine, worry is etched in his features.

"What?" I demand.

He swallows and reaches for my hand. "What happened with Diego?"

I frantically pull open the glove box, where I'd shoved some crackers for emergencies, and attempt to stall by eating. When I don't answer him and instead munch on the snack, he lets out a sigh and reverses the truck. By the time we reach his townhouse at the end of the street, I've nearly downed the entire sleeve of crackers to avoid spilling the icky details of "Daddy" Diego. As soon as he puts the car in park, I launch out and hightail it up to the house. Cars are parked every-where and people in costumes are heading to the front door.

I'm almost to the porch when someone grabs my arm.

I yelp out in surprise.

"It's me," Ren assures me. He comes to stand in front of me and scowls. "Tell me. Something bad happened. Something you didn't even tell your dad. You need to tell me."

I purse my lips together. "Why?" A shudder passes through me.

"Because something happened to you, goddammit. I need to know…" he trails off and runs his fingers through his hair, messing up his 80s hair style. "I need to know what happened and who I need to kill." His glare is severe. If this were old Ren, I would have laughed after such a proclamation. New Ren is serious.

"I had it handled," I lie. I was scared shitless when I thought he was going to rape me. I'd gotten myself into something that was way over my head.

"Did he touch you?" he demands, his jaw ticking with fury.

I swallow down my emotion and shake my head. "No."

His eyes narrow as he studies me. "I don't believe you."

Tearing my gaze from his, I shrug my shoulders. "I'm sorry." I run past a group of people and push through the front door. Luciana and Calder really went all out decorating the place. There's food too. My stomach grumbles with delight but I charge past the kitchen toward the bedrooms. Once I make my way into Ren's, I make a run for the bathroom. I've barely shut the door when it's being pushed back open.

My eyes flip up to the mirror. Ren stands behind me looking more like the bad guy in the 80s movies than the good guy. And I look absolutely ridiculous in a tiger outfit that's two sizes too small. He places his large hands on my hips and twists me to face him.

"Tell me."

I purse my lips together and pout. "You're being a bully."

He winces and I instantly feel bad. Then, his fingers are under my chin, lifting it up so he can look into my eyes.

"I'm not sorry for worrying about you. You may be all fierce and tough and have claws, but people can still hurt you. For that reason alone, I'll always fucking stress out about you." He leans forward and drops a soft kiss on my lips. "Have you told anyone?"

Emotion clogs my throat and I fight tears. "N-No."

"No secrets, Brie. Bring it into the light. We'll face it together."

My chest aches but I know he's right. I don't want to carry that burden alone. He's always been the one I can confide in. "He was just going to take what he wanted..."

He stiffens, and I can sense the rage bubbling from him, yet he somehow manages to remain quiet.

I continue, my voice slightly wobbling. "We made a deal. But then..." I choke out. "I thought he was going to rape me. He overpowered me and he...and he..."

"So help me, Brie, I'm going to cut out his fucking throat," he growls in a low, threatening tone.

"But he didn't." I drop my voice to a whisper. A tear sneaks out and I worry if it'll smear my cat whiskers. "He just exerted his power over me is all. I felt helpless and alone. I was in over my head with him. He could have...if he wanted...." Thank God he didn't.

A roar, louder than any sound my tiger of a husband ever made, rips from Ren. His entire body ripples with fury. I hug his middle so he doesn't do anything stupid, like destroy his bathroom. "You're not alone. Not anymore."

"Then he took the necklace you gave me and Duvan's wedding ring." At this statement, I burst into tears.

His strong arms hug me tight. For the longest time, he doesn't speak a word. "Gabe doesn't know those details, I'm guessing?"

"Daddy had already gotten his ass beat all to hell that day. If he'd known Diego was anything other than pure business with me, he'd have gotten himself killed," I say softly.

He grips my sleek ponytail and tugs until I'm looking up at him. "I'll keep you safe from those motherfuckers," he vows. "You're going to get away from that crooked life. Here, you're going to have a normal one. You're going to take care of those babies without having to look over your shoulder. Brie," he murmurs and dips his head down, "you're safe here."

His lips crash against mine.

When we finally pull away from our soul consuming kiss, he regards me with a fierce look on his face. "Be careful tonight."

I nod and give him a smile. He grabs my hand and we leave his room to go back into the fray of people dancing and drinking in his house. I see lots of cool costumes but Ren's is the best hands down. Only he could make looking like an 80s nerd seem so hot. I'm smiling as we enter the kitchen where Calder and Luciana are putting on a show. A puppet show that is. The sight is hysterical—her looking like a dummy with his hand up under the back of her shirt. Both of them are all smiles as they perform their little show.

"Oh my God," I shout over the music to Ren. "What is even happening there right now?"

He chuckles and pulls me to his side. "Whatever it is,

they're both happy to do it. Did you know Luciana thinks my brother looks like Justin Bieber?"

I snort and nod. "I don't see it."

Ren smirks at me. "He does kinds look like a douchebag, so maybe she's on to something."

He pulls away from me to pour me some Pepsi into a red Solo cup. I notice he abstains from the alcohol too. Not sure if it's in solidarity with me because of the pregnancy or if it's because he wants to remain alert. By the way his eyes skim the crowd every so often and he keeps me within touching distance lets me know it's the latter. As much as Diego terrifies me and as much as Esteban haunts my every thought, I doubt either one of them would be so bold as to come to this party. Hell, for all I know, they're probably still in Colombia. I don't feel threatened right now. For once, I feel kind of normal. A young adult at a party full of college-aged people who are dressed up and drinking and laughing. Ren has always wanted a simple, happy life for me. One where I was free to make my own choices and do my own thing. I've been here a week and he's already done so much to help make that happen.

"I'm going to run to the restroom," I tell him.

His features harden, but the last thing I want is for him to follow me to pee. "I can stand outside the door."

Shaking my head, I put my palm on his firm chest and stand on my toes. Our lips brush against each other briefly. I did it. I kissed him in front of others for the first time. His big hands slide to my ass and he pulls me flush against him.

"That was only a tease," he murmurs, his hot breath tickling my lips. "That will never be enough."

He kisses me hard enough to steal my breath and pull a moan from me. When I finally manage to free myself from his magnetic touch, he flashes me a knowing smirk. I laugh and stick my tongue out before heading to the bathroom. I'm just about to twist the knob to the front bathroom when the door flies open. The bathroom is dark from the lights being cut off, so all I get is a flash of blonde pigtails before she brushes up against me. I notice her belly is huge with pregnancy. When I lift my gaze, I meet curious blue eyes.

Familiar.

I open my mouth to speak but she grips my elbows and drags me into the bathroom. She shuts the door behind her and blocks my path to it. The lock clicks as the light turns back on.

I'm staring at Harley Quinn. Well, not the *real* Harley Quinn—The Joker's insane girlfriend—from the *Suicide Squad* movie. But someone who's nailed her costume with precision. The real-live version might be a little more frightening than the character from the movie though.

Blonde pigtails with streaks of pink and blue. Bright red lipstick on a devious grin. She wears a white T-shirt that says "Daddy's Lil Monster" that has been shredded, revealing her very pregnant belly. Tiny red and blue sequined shorts sparkle in the light.

But what's alarming is the baseball bat she's holding.

"Gabriella," she says, a small bite to her voice that has my hackles rising. She smacks on her gum as she takes her time sizing me up.

I'm too frozen in fear to move.

"Hannah," I choke out. My voice is barely a whisper. When she lifts the baseball bat and runs her hand over it, I flinch and protectively clutch at my stomach.

Calculating eyes dart to my midsection and her hard

gaze softens. "You pregnant?" she questions as she lets the bat swing lazily beside her like a pendulum. Then, she blows a bubble with her pink gum.

A cold sweat breaks out over my flesh. The terror has swallowed me whole. This woman cut open my mother's throat and ran off with my father. For years, I imagined how this conversation would go. How I would scream at her and rip her hair out. How I would make her pay for what she did to Mom. I never imagined I'd be so scared of her.

"P-Please don't hurt me," I utter. "Or my babies."

At this, her eyes widen with glee and that sends my heart thumping right out of my chest.

"Twins?" She beams at me as if this is the coolest thing she's ever heard.

Swallowing, I nod. My eyes quickly dart around the room in search of a weapon. Calder and Ren don't keep weapons in their bathroom. I decide right then and there that if I make it out of this bathroom alive, my house will have hidden weapons in all the rooms.

"I'm pregnant." She rubs her belly and smacks her gum. "Second baby. Your brother."

I inch away from her because I don't like how she keeps swinging the bat, the arc growing wider and wider. "That's nice," I blurt out.

She flashes me another grin. "Do you ever get cravings?"

I blink at her in confusion. "Uh, not really. Mostly I try not to be sick. I eat a lot of peanut butter crackers."

Her head bobs up and down knowingly. "Morning sickness is the worst. Try keeping some saltines by your bed and eat a couple before you even get up. That way, you have something on your stomach when you go to eat something a little more substantial."

Pregnancy advice from my...psycho, murdering stepmother.

"Thanks." I chew on my bottom lip and look past her to the door. Surely any minute Ren will come looking for me. "I really need to pee. Do you think you could—"

She charges for me and all I can do is squeak. My palms go in the air in a defensive move. I expect the baseball bat to crack me over the head but it doesn't. Her belly presses against mine wedging me between her and the wall. All humor and sweetness is gone as she glares down at me.

"He told me what happened," she snaps, fury flickering in her steely blue eyes that look more fierce than her brother's ever could be.

"W-Who? What?" I stammer, my heart thundering to the point of pain.

She reaches her hand up and I flinch. Her red lips purse into a line as she pets me—fucking pets me like I'm a little kitten. "Gabe. He told me about him."

"Who?"

"Estebaaaaaaan," she hisses through clenched teeth.

I'm thoroughly confused at this point. I don't understand her misplaced rage.

"He," she snarls as her mouth gets close to my ear, "raped you."

Shuddering, I let out a sob. I'm confused when this psychopath hugs me rather than hurts me. I stand still, afraid to move or speak. She releases me and glares at me.

"He'll pay for what he did. That's what happens to rapists." Her eyes narrow. "They pay with their life."

Anger, my most recent familiar emotion, finally claws

up inside of me from whatever depths it was hiding in. "And what do murderers pay with?" I don't remind her that my father and Hannah's husband, according to Baylee, is also a rapist. She's proven once that she will kill the ones I love. The last thing I want is for her to snap and kill Daddy too.

Her blue eyes soften and she gives me a shy grin that makes my insides quake with more fear. "Oh, baby girl, I was just curious."

I scoff and fist my hands. "Curious?" My tone is shrill. "Your fucking curiosity killed my mother?!"

She shrugs her shoulders but then levels me with another one of her scary stares. "And the fact that she was in my way. Are you in my way?"

A threat.

"Unbelievable," I hiss. "How are you even cut from the same cloth as Ren?"

At the mention of his name, she smiles sweetly at me. "Take care of my brother and I'll take care of your father." Then the smile melts away. "Hurt my brother and I'll hurt you."

"Fuck you, crazy!" I screech. "You killed my mother!"

She points the bat at me. "In the past, baby girl."

Shaking my head, I start for her but she pokes the bat in the center of my chest stopping me. "I'm sorry," she hisses. "Okay? I didn't know it would hurt so many people. It was an accident, kinda. Just know if I could go back, I wouldn't do it again."

A flicker of deception in her gaze tells me that's a lie.

"Just go. I don't ever want to see you again," I tell her, my voice ragged. I'm exhausted from this little run in.

She drops the bat back down to her side and once again

143

sizes me up, her gaze lingering on my rounded stomach. "Fine. I'll stay away. But remember what I said."

My brows drag together in confusion.

"Rapists pay with their life," she spits out. "That's a motherfucking promise, baby girl." She blows another bubble and then waves. When she opens the bathroom door, Ren stands on the other side with his hand poised to knock. It takes him three seconds to take in the scene before him before he's charging inside and has his sister by the throat. I've never seen him so furious.

The bat clangs to the floor as she grabs at his wrist. He walks her to the wall beside me and gets right in her face.

"You're not welcome here," he snaps, his entire body quaking with rage.

"Let her go." Daddy's voice from the bathroom doorway is strained. Tired even.

My gaze flits over to him. He's dressed in dark jeans and a black leather jacket with a dark red colored scarf around his neck that's tucked into his jacket. His chocolate-colored hair has been tousled and styled differently than usual. It's his weapon that scares the shit out me. Who twists barbed wire around a wooden baseball bat?

"Hey puddin," Hannah chokes out. All psychopathic looks are gone. She regards my father as if he's the sun and she wants to bask in his warmth.

Ren releases Hannah and points at the door. "Brie, go to my room and lock the door. I'll be there in a minute."

I give him a nod and start past Daddy. Before I pass him, though, I point at his costume. "Who are you supposed to be, anyway?"

He smirks. "I am Negan."

144

"Who?"

"The Walking Dea—"

"Brie. Now," Ren interrupts with a barely contained growl.

I push past Daddy and leave Ren to deal with them. Once I slip into Ren's room and lock the door behind me, I kick off my flats and head toward the bathroom. I finish my business, which I never even got to start because I ran into that crazy woman, and then quickly wash away my smeared makeup.

Another shudder ripples through me as realization sets in. I was alone in the bathroom with my mother's killer. And she was fucking terrifying. I don't understand, after knowing Ren and Calder and then later meeting their mother, how Hannah is even a part of their family. They're all so normal and she's so…scary.

I peel off the stupid cat suit until I'm in nothing but my panties. Walking over to the closet, I catch my reflection in the mirror. My hands are trembling and I'm wearing a grim expression. This whole run in with her has wiped me out. I locate a T-shirt of Ren's from his closet—which swallows me up—before turning off the lights and crawling into his bed. Light from the cracked bathroom door streams in and doesn't leave me totally in the dark.

I'm distracted by my thoughts when I think I see the closet door move. Terror skitters over me like a thousand bugs on the move.

"Who's there?" I demand, sitting up.

The door swings open and a blur charges toward me. I've barely opened my mouth to scream when a large hand clamps over it. His other hand manages to collect both my wrists and pin them to the bed. The giant man's heavy body presses against me and his hot breaths warm my face. I start to fight my attacker, whose face is hidden by shadows until he speaks.

"Stop freaking out," he growls. "It's me."

The familiar voice slices right through me. His voice confuses me. It's deeper and lower than I remember. Harsher. I squint in the darkness to try and take in his features. All I can see is the outline of his head. His hair is longer than before.

"Miss me?" The normally playful tone in his voice is gone. It feels forced.

Swallowing, I give a clipped nod and when he lets go of my mouth, I speak. "Ozzy, where have you been?"

He relaxes but doesn't release me. I squirm but he ignores the movement. "I've been putting out fires," he snips out. "Fires *you* started."

I once again wriggle in his grasp. "You're hurting me," I lie. "Why are you holding me down?"

He huffs. "I'm holding you down because I want to talk to you and I don't need you running off to your little boyfriend."

I chew on my bottom lip. Ren will be in here at any moment. Things could get ugly quick. "He's not my boyfriend." Another lie. But is it? My mind squashes the thought because now is not the time to analyze me and Ren's relationship status.

"Sure looked like your boyfriend when you were sucking face in the kitchen earlier," he bites out. "How long did you wait before you moved on? Was my brother's body even cold yet, Brie?"

I choke at his words and if my hands were free, I'd slap him.

"Fuck you!" I screech. "Let go of me!"

146

At one time, I used to enjoy Ozzy's playfulness. How we'd cuddle up in bed and laugh. How he'd touch me as close friends often do. Nothing about the way he's touching me now is playful.

"Just tell me why it is you couldn't even make sure my brother was dead first before you moved on to Ren. I thought you were my friend. Hell, I even thought he was my friend. Were you two fucking behind Duvan's back the whole time?" he demands.

This time, I do manage to free my hand. And as I wanted to do the first time, I smack the shit out of him. He lets out a snarl as he pins it back to the mattress.

"Just answer the goddamned question," he snaps.

I spit at him. "You know that's not the truth. I loved your brother."

His grip loosens and he sags against me. My angry friend chokes on his emotion. "I had to watch. Jesus Christ, I can't get that image of Heath cutting him open out of my head." He burrows his face against my hair and inhales me. "I missed you, Brie. Everything has gone to shit."

Guilt crawls its way up my spine. Oscar lost Duvan too. He's hurting just as much as I am. This time, when my hands are released, I slide them around his back to hug him.

"You've started a war," he murmurs. "I don't know how to fix any of it. I'm supposed to be here…I'm supposed to…" he trails off. "My father wants me to…but I just can't. God, I've missed you."

Fear clutches at my throat. "W-What did Camilo want you to do?"

"To come get you. So he could *discuss* what you did with Duvan's territory." He starts sniffling but true to Oscar, his hands start roaming and his mouth is on the flesh below my ear. "You're not safe. He'll hurt you."

I freeze at his words just as his hand slips under my shirt. He starts kissing my neck and when he presses his hardness against my thigh, I'm jolted to reality.

"Oscar," I groan, trying to push his heavy body away. "Get off me. We need to talk about this."

His palm grips my sore breast and I let out a yelp of surprise. I'm still ordering him to get off me when I hear a noise and then Oscar's weight is ripped off my body. Ren's face is positively murderous as he rears back his fist. Then, I hear a crunch. Ozzy crumples to the floor with a groan. Ren's furious glare meets mine, assessing me for damage for a quick moment, before he lunges at Oscar.

*Crunch.*

*Crunch.*

*Crunch.*

He gets three solid punches in on Ozzy before I snap out of my daze and scramble after him. I manage to slide my arms around Ren's middle to pull him away.

"I'm okay," I tell him. "Please stop hitting him."

Ren is tense as hell but he allows me to pull him away from a now bloodied Oscar. We both sit on our asses on the carpet. Ren's shoulders hunch forward as I hug him from behind.

"He...he was..." he trails off.

"It looked worse than it was," I assure him. "I promise."

When Oscar manages to get up on his hands and knees, Ren tenses again.

"Remember what I said," Ozzy murmurs as he wipes his nose with the back of his hand. "You're not safe. I just wanted to talk to you about that and about Vee—"

"You're never talking to her again," Ren roars and rises to his feet, despite my clutching for him. I'm left on the floor as he towers over Ozzy who clumsily gets back on his feet.

Ozzy shoots me a desperate look with one eye. The other one is already swelling shut. "Please…"

"Where's Vee?" I demand, a quiver of worry shuddering through me.

Oscar hunches as he lets out a howl of frustration. "I don't know for sure but…"

Ren pulls me against his side and I'm assuming it's because if he's not holding me then he'll have the urge to beat Oscar's face in some more.

"I think she might be with Esteban," Oscar growls. Then his voice cracks. "Unwillingly."

# XIII | Ren

**"S**TOP PACING." BRIE'S VOICE CUTS THROUGH MY MENTAL anguish, and I give her a sharp look.

"I can't help it," I snap. "These people just won't leave you the fuck alone."

She tugs her towel from her body and starts drying her wet hair with it. After Oscar stumbled from my room, I gathered her up and took her back to her house. Where there weren't a million people. Where I could turn on the alarm and keep her safe.

"He didn't hurt me," she tells me. Her tits bounce as she towel dries her mane. I become momentarily distracted and find myself staring at them.

She lets out a small chuckle and approaches me where I'm pacing manically at the end of her bed. Her towel drops to the floor and then she grabs for mine that's tied around my waist. I let out a groan when she pulls it away. Then it's just us. Naked and together.

"Ren," she coos. "Stop stressing out. I'm okay."

I frown down at her. "Camilo is out there. Diego is out there. Fucking Esteban is out there. They all want something from you. You are *not* okay."

A dark look swims across her features. "So we'll figure it out. But I won't live my life in fear," she tells me with a huff.

I slide my fingers into her wet hair and tilt her head up so I can inspect her perfect features. "You were alone in that bathroom with my whack job baseball bat wielding sister. I'm fucking afraid for you. Don't be naïve, Brie. There are monsters everywhere."

Her nostrils flare and she pushes against my chest but I still have a grip on her hair. "Thinking about them twenty-four-seven solves nothing!"

I slide one hand to the front of her throat and capture her jaw in my fingertips. My lips ghost over hers. "But burying your head in the sand won't make it go away either," I growl. I nip at her bottom lip.

"You're bossy and rude. Where's my sweet Ren?" she huffs but then lets out a moan when I suckle on the lip I was just abusing. Her palms, which were pushing on my chest, have started to slide south where my cock is hard and at attention.

"He died."

She freezes at my words, and I instantly feel like a dick.

"I'm sorry—"

A fierce roar escapes her as she shoves me, breaking our connection. I expect to have to chase after her. Not for her to start attacking me. Her tiny fists beat against my chest as she lets out her emotions.

"Don't even say shit like that to me! You're the only person I have left who I can truly count on! I'm scared too but I'll go mental if I stress about it all damn day!" With each hit to my chest, she pushes me farther back until my ass is against the wall. She delivers a particularly powerful blow to my stomach that has my breath hissing out. I slide my palms to her ass and lift her up before pushing my body between her thighs. I twist us around until it's her back pressed against the wall. Another shift and my cock slides easily into her tight cunt. We both freeze for a moment.

"I said I'm sorry," I utter and thrust into her hard enough for her head to bounce against the wall.

She grips at my wet hair and lets out a hiss. "Apology accepted. Now harder."

Our lips bump against each other as I drive into her pussy with powerful thrusts. Her angry yet needy mewls urge me on. I fuck her against the wall so fast and so hard that a picture falls off and crashes to the floor. All that can be heard is the slapping of skin, desperate sounds we're both making, and the occasional bump of her head against the wall. When she lets out a scream that sounds like my name and rips at my hair, I lose it. Her pussy clutches my dick so hard I see stars. With a groan, I release my seed into her. My mouth seals against hers so I can breathe in her sounds of pleasure. The moment we both come down from our high, I walk her over to the bed. I lie her flat on her back and begin trailing soft kisses all over her full tits. Then, I make my way south.

She lets out a hiss when my mouth covers her mound. I lap at our juices running out of her and taste what only our lovemaking creates. Salty and musky and us.

"I can't believe you're doing that," she murmurs, her body jolting on the bed.

I nip at her clit and then run my tongue back down her seam to her opening. "We taste good, baby. I could spend all night licking every part of you."

She moans and spreads her legs further apart. "I want you to. I like your tongue on me. In me."

With a growl, because her sexy as hell words turn me on, I push her thighs until they're pressed against her belly. I drag my tongue lower teasing another delicious part of her.

"Ren…I don't know…" she utters but doesn't try to stop me.

Undeterred, I spread her ass cheeks apart and run the tip of my tongue along the puckered hole. She gasps and wriggles but doesn't tell me no. My tongue meets resistance, but I manage to breach the tight hole. I hear my name on her lips that quickly turns into a chant as I fuck her this way. While I taste her in such a foreign place, I pinch and rub her clit. It doesn't take long for her to cry out as she comes again. Gently, I tug my tongue free from her bottom and breathe against the tender flesh.

"I'm going to put my cock there next. Tell me no, Brie." I bite the inside of her ass cheek and she gasps. "You're fragile and broken and your heart is in shreds. Yet…" I groan and then press a soft kiss to her pussy. "I want to fuck and defile you. I want to see you forget it all as you lose yourself to unknown pleasure. I know it's too much for you. You deserve gentle. You deserve love and respect. And all I want to do is fuck you raw while you chant my motherfucking name. You asked where your sweet Ren is," I groan as I grab her hips. "Truth is, I don't know. I don't care either. All I care about is you. Being inside you. Taking care of you. Fucking and claiming and loving you." Our eyes meet and her hooded eyes glimmer with emotion. My fingers dig into her hips as I roll her over onto her stomach. "I'm not the man you deserve." I suck on my finger before teasing her asshole with it. "But I'm the man you're going to get." She lets out a low moan into the pillow when I push my longest digit into her ass. "Tell me no, baby. Tell me you need me to take you in there and bathe you and whisper sweet nothings in your ear." I drive my finger in and out of her tightness.

She reaches for her night table and yanks open the drawer. When she grabs the bottle of lube we've been using on occasion, my rock hard cock bounces in excitement. I let out a growl as I slip my finger from her and take the bottle. Pouring a healthy amount on my dick, I rub it in to thoroughly lubricate it before using the excess to prime her opening.

"Last chance. Tell me you need it sweet," I murmur.

On shaky arms and legs, she rises to her knees and elbows. "I need you to fuck me. Hard."

An animalistic sound rasps from me as I grab on to her sexy hip with one hand and use the other hand to help push the tip of my dick inside her tightest hole. She fists the blankets while simultaneously letting out a groan when I begin easing into her.

"Say no," I beg, my voice shaking. The pleasure is too much.

"Claim me, Ren McPherson. Fucking claim me."

Her scream isn't one of pain or horror or fear. It's raw, carnal pleasure as I do exactly as she wishes. I drive into her without apology. My death grip on her hips will leave bruises. Her ass will be sore for days. But right now, none of that matters as I stake claim on this woman.

"You're mine," I snarl, my hips bucking hard against her.

"Yours," she moans in agreement against the blanket. "Yours."

I brush my fingertips over her clit and it's enough to send her over the edge. Her ass contracts around my cock, causing me to go blind with bliss that is only associated with Brie.

Gabriella Rojas is mine.

Fucking finally.

I'm awoken in the middle of the night when I hear Brie whimper in her sleep. She calls out Duvan's name, which makes my stomach twist into a knot. I hate that she's having a nightmare. The way she says his name is the exact same way she called out for him when he bled out right before her eyes on that fateful day.

"Shhh," I murmur against her hair. "I'm here."

My words don't wake her but she does calm. Her fingernails dig into my pectoral as she seems to hang on for dear life. When her breathing evens out again, I drift off thinking about one of our first dates.

*"He likes her," I tell her and point off in the distance where Calder chases Vee down the beach.*

*Brie looks up at me with a sweet smile. "She likes him." Even though her reply is about my brother and her friend, I can't help but wonder if there is a double meaning.*

*"He thinks she's beautiful. So fucking beautiful," I murmur as I take both her hands.*

*Her black eyelashes flutter and her cheeks turn rosy. "She thinks he's pretty good looking as well."*

*I release one hand and gently grip her jaw. I tilt her head up so I can look into her deep chocolate eyes, that hide a past that hurts. I'm dying to learn every part of her and take away some of that hurt.* "He wants to kiss her."

*Her lips part and her eyes close.* "She wants him to kiss her."

*I smile and then drop my lips to hers. Her soft mouth is like a shot of vodka on a cold day. It sends surges of warmth shooting through me. With a groan, I deepen our innocent kiss. The taste of her tongue is sweet and so damn delicious. Her fingers grip my T-shirt as she pulls me closer. What started out as gentle, quickly becomes ravenous. She clutches on to me as if she never wants to let go. I don't want that to ever happen. This girl...she's mine. No way around it.*

*When I finally release her lips, she's breathless. Her arms wrap around my middle and I hug her against my chest. I like her right here. I'm never going to get enough of her.*

One day she'll find out your secret.

*The thought hits me like a Mack truck. All hope for a normal relationship with this girl flies out the window. Truth is, if she ever finds out who I am...exactly what role I play in her world, she'll hate me. God, I don't want her to hate me.*

*She'll never know, as long as I have anything to do with it.*

*I'm brooding over the stupid predicament my selfish sister put me in when Brie looks up at me. All inner fury at my sister melts away as this girl beams at me. Her smile is enough to chase away any and all dark thoughts. Her smile is perfect.*

"She wants him to kiss her again," *she tells me with a shy grin.*

*I smirk at her.* "He's going to do whatever it takes to make her happy."

I'm jolted from the past when Brie once again murmurs a name. This time it's mine and she doesn't sound pained.

Fierce male pride fills my chest as I hold her tight against me and kiss her hair. I know I will spend my life doing whatever it takes to dissolve her stress and worries.

*He's going to do whatever it takes to make her happy.*

# XIV | Brie

I WAKE UP IN THE WEE HOURS OF THE MORNING TO REN'S finger lazily tracing lines on my bare stomach. The intimate way in which he does it has my heart flopping wildly in my chest. For the first time since I lost Duvan, I feel a sense of peace. Like maybe, just maybe, I can one day be happy. And with Ren, it certainly feels possible.

His dark hair is messy from sleep and his eyes are still closed, but the small smile on his face tells me he's awake. I try not to let on that I'm awake so I can watch him. My world has been nothing but chaos for months. Even with Duvan, I always had a sense of worry surrounding me.

Right now, though…

In this exact moment…

I am relaxed.

My world is quiet and I want to savor it.

I find myself staring at Ren's full lips. Dark hair is growing on his face—hair that never existed when we dated what seems like eons ago. His new look makes him seem edgier.

Slightly rugged. All man. I like that he seems a little unkempt and no longer guided by rules and order. He left his home because of me. Because his twisted sister staying there was an insult to me. It may seem like something small but it means a lot to me. More than he'll ever know.

His palm splays out over my belly and my breath hitches. I like that he's curious about my stomach and how he sometimes talks to the babies. If Duvan were here, I know it would be what he'd do. In a selfish way, I'm glad these little ones have someone who cares, besides me. And Ren does care. He does more than care.

He loves me.

The thought makes my heart clench. Ren has loved me for a long time. That never went away. Even when I was off loving someone else, Ren was here, his entire heart beating for me. The thought of him longing for me while I was gone causes my eyes to burn with tears. Nothing about how our relationship ended before was fair.

"Why are you crying?"

I blink away the blur and find steely blue eyes boring into me. Those eyes. So loving and fierce and undeterred. I get lost in them a lot lately. Those eyes make me feel safe.

"No reason," I lie as I run my fingers through his unruly hair.

His eyebrows furl together and he leans forward to brush a kiss against my cheek. "You're lying. Tell me what has you upset this morning. I want to fix it."

Those words only make the tears fall more freely. I let out a ragged breath of emotion as I try desperately not to cry. Being pregnant has my normally tough exterior reduced to flimsy shreds. He kisses my wet cheek as if to encourage me.

"I can't ever love you like I loved him," I blurt out, my voice hard despite the tears. There. I said it.

His body tenses and his fingertips that had been tracing lines on my belly stop. As soon as the words pierce the quiet air, I want to reel them back in and tuck them back in the dark parts of my head where they belong. Those words cut. And the last thing I want to do is cut Ren. But not being honest will only build what we have on lies and untruths.

I expect him to get upset. To yell or accuse me of leading him on. Something. Instead, he simply resumes tracing his finger on my stomach again. I bite on my bottom lip as I wait for him to say something. His brows are still pinched together and his gaze is somewhere else in the room as if he's lost in thought. After what feels like forever, he sits up on one elbow and reaches for my tattooed wrist.

Our eyes meet and he gives me such a sweet smile, it makes my chest ache. His thumb swipes over my wrist before he pulls it to his lips. Hot breath tickles my flesh and then he kisses the heart tattoo with another man's name on it.

"Your heart…"

"Is torn and useless and not much of it is left."

His lips press to my flesh again as his blue eyes dart to mine, locking on me. "It's still your heart. It still deserves love."

A tear streaks down my cheek and my bottom lip wobbles. "What if I don't have any love left to give? What if it's always just partial and clouded and obstructed? How can you love someone who will never be able to reciprocate fully?" I slide my palm to his cheek and he leans into my touch as if I'm the magnet he can't help but be attracted to.

"That's simple, baby," he says with an easy grin. "I'll love enough for the both of us. My heart is big enough to hold yours." His hand rubs my stomach again. "My heart is big enough to love all of you."

At this, I begin to full on sob. He pulls me to his chest and I mold myself against his strong body. I'm warmed when he kisses my forehead.

"Brie," he tells me, his voice low and gravelly. "You're it for me. You always have been. I lost you once and I won't lose you again. If all you can give me are broken parts, I'll fucking take them because they're still you. Broken or not, the girl I remember from that window all those years ago still exists. I'll weather whatever storms that hit *for you*. I want to keep you safe and see you smile again. Let me love you. I'm not asking for anything in return."

I hug his middle but don't speak right away. I don't trust myself not to break down into a million pieces.

"If it were possible to love again," I finally say, my voice ragged and but a whisper. "It would be with you. I'll always try for you. I just hope that it will be enough."

He chuckles and his long fingers stroke the outside of my arm, making me shiver. "Having you right here, right now, is enough. You'll always be more than I ever expected."

I slide my hand lower down his ridiculously toned stomach until my fingertip traces his dark trail of hair that disappears under the sheet. His cock jolts under the covers and it makes me smile. "Make love to me," I murmur and slip my hand under the fabric to grip his nice cock. "I want to feel the love you insist on giving me."

A growl rumbles from him as he rolls over on top of me. His lips begin peppering kisses all over my face. He does it in such a playful way, I find myself giggling and running off the last of my tears. Our eyes meet and his blaze intensely with his dedication to me. My laughter dies the moment he pushes his cock into me.

He rests on one elbow as he slowly rocks into me. The other hand whispers touches all over my breast, throat, face, and hair. His worshipping touch repairs parts of my broken soul. The way he stares at me as if I'm the only thing in this world has me praying to God that I can one day be the woman he deserves. I'll try. For Ren, I'll try. Because if anyone deserves all-encompassing selfless love, it's Ren McPherson.

"You're beautiful," he murmurs.

I smile at him. "So are you."

He smirks and thrusts a little harder into me. "Guys prefer the term 'sexy as fuck' but beautiful will do. Just remember for next time." He winks at me before diving in to nip at my throat.

"Definitely sexy as fuck," I agree but trail off with a moan. The way he grinds against me delivers pleasure to my clit. It's exhilarating and I want all that he has to give me.

Our love making quickly becomes ravenous. What started off as gentle soon becomes grunts and groans and growls. Fingernails and teeth scraping flesh. Begging and pleading for release.

"I love you, Brie," he murmurs against the shell of my ear. The words, even though I'm not sure I'll ever be able to say them back, send me over the edge. My eyes close as an intense soul healing orgasm sears through me. His heat pours into me, chasing my release. A few more thrusts and he nuzzles against me, reminding me of an animal caring for his mate.

The tigress may have lost her tiger.

But this tigress is *not* alone.

After a moment, he sits up so he can look down at me. A panty-melting grin spreads across his most definitely *sexy-as-fuck* face.

"I'm going to wash your pretty ass in the shower and then…" he trails off as he looks down between us. "I'm going to feed you and the babies. Waffles covered in whipped butter and warm syrup. Maybe a side of strawberries. What do you think?" He waggles his brows at me.

I laugh and lock away the perfect moment with him in my memory for whenever I have a sad day. This memory will most definitely make me happy.

"I think you're going to make me orgasm again," I tease.

His cock twitches inside me. "Oh," he says with a wolfish smile. "I can make that happen before we even leave this bed."

A growl on his part is my only warning before he makes good on his promise.

"The question is," I say as calmly as I can. "Will you be able to find her?"

Ren's father, War, looks up from his laptop and frowns. "I'm sure as hell going to try." War has a gentleness about him that had me relaxing almost as soon as I met him. Maybe it's that he looks so much like Ren, and Ren equals safety in my mind. Either way, I just like him.

An entire week has passed since Oscar came to see me and it's eating me alive. Vee's missing. She's not at a spa like I'd hoped. She's gone. Oscar still won't take my calls, but I did receive some texts from him over the week to which he never replied when I answered back.

**Ozzy: Her car is at her parents' house, but I broke in. She's not there.**

**Ozzy: The apartment was empty too.**

**Ozzy: Nothing seems out of sorts except that she's just gone. My father claims innocence but I'm not sure.**

**Ozzy: My father wants me to meet with Diego. I'm supposed to take our territory back. How the fuck am I supposed to do that?**

**Ozzy: If Diego has her, I'll gut him.**

**Ozzy: My father got a call from Esteban but won't tell me what he said. I think it may involve you.**

None of his texts made much sense, but they have my anxiety on high. Ren seems to notice my rigid shoulders because he walks up behind the chair at my kitchen table and rubs on my neck.

"Did Oscar mention anymore about Esteban?" Daddy questions from across the table. Toto has fallen asleep in his arms and he absently strokes at her blonde curls. She clutches onto her favored Veggie Tales stuffed animal, Larry the Cucumber. My sister is so sweet and innocent. If she didn't represent the psycho who killed my mother, I'd be warmed by the sight of her looking so serene in our daddy's arms. But the chill always remains.

"No," I say with a sigh. "His texts are sporadic at best. That's why we need to find Vee. Ozzy is too distracted by what his father is making him do. I'm afraid she might be hurt somewhere."

War taps away at his computer but speaks. "I've looked up all of her credit cards. All activity ceases the day after…" His blue eyes dart to mine, and I see pity in them. "Anyway, all activity stops. Same with her mother. Neither of them has purchased a thing since then. I've hacked into their bank accounts. All the money they had is still there. Everything is just sitting."

"What about Esteban?" Daddy demands. "Can you find where the hell he's been holed up? He and I need to have some words." Rage ripples from him. The crazed look on his face reminds me of a demon. And the fact that he's holding a blonde little cherub in his arms only makes the whole thing seem a little more comical.

"Maybe I could ask Diego and—"

"Fuck no!" Both Daddy and Ren growl at the same time.

War gives me a supportive smile and a wink—one that says he'll research Diego and follow any leads. I give him a slight nod before grabbing Ren's hand. When I look up at him, he's gazing at me with such love and fierce protection, I almost waver under it.

"Can you get me something to drink?" I ask. "I'm not feeling so well."

He gives me a nod and then presses a kiss to my head. Once he leaves, I find Daddy and War watching me. I'm still not used to me and Ren's relationship being public, but it is. Nobody, except for Oscar, has criticized us for it either. As much as Ozzy's words had broken my heart, I refuse to feel guilty for letting Ren into my heart. Truth is, he never left. Ren is my best friend and my protector. My lover and a million other things all rolled up into one person. When I vowed a week ago that I belonged to him, I meant it. He may only get a broken sliver of who I used to be, but that's all I have to give.

Daddy and War get into a heated discussion about the "Colombian cunts" as my dad calls them. My phone buzzes in my lap and I quickly lift it up to see if it's Ozzy with any news.

**Unknown Number: We need to talk, cariño. Privately. I have something you want, remember? And I need something from you.**

Ice slides through my veins, freezing me in my seat. With shaky hands, I quickly type out a response.

**Me: Talk with you ends up with you trying to either fuck me or fuck me over.**

He buzzes back immediately.

**Unknown Number: Camilo is on my ass. Tell me where you live and I'll come see you.**

**Me: Absolutely fucking not. We meet in public or we don't meet at all.**

**Unknown Number: I'm here in San Diego. There's a restaurant at one of the piers. Come alone and I'll give you your precious jewelry back. I'm not going to hurt you. Daddy Diego swears on his big dick.**

I suppress a shiver at the thought of him here in my city.

"Does Oscar have any news?" Daddy questions, jerking me away from my inner shuddering over the thought of Diego's dick. His eyes dart to my phone. I hold it to my chest.

"Uh," I murmur. "Nope."

His eyes narrow and he gives War a pointed look that I'm not meant to interpret. It annoys me. When they go back to discussing how Daddy plans on murdering the whole lot of them, I look back down at my phone and tap away my response.

**Me: Fine. Get me the address. I'll shoot you if you try anything funny.**

**Unknown Number: I have no doubts, cariño. We both know you've got bigger balls than most men. Meet me in**

**an hour. Wear something sexy. I want to see your nipples through your clothes.**

I quickly delete the horndog's texts and then bite on my bottom lip. I'm about to have to lie to these guys.

"Everything okay?" Ren questions from behind me causing me to jump. I nod quickly—too quickly—and take the glass of Sprite from him. In several gulps, I down half the glass.

"I'm fine but I was going to go over to your house for a bit and see Luciana," I lie. "May I borrow your truck?"

He frowns. "Let me get the keys and I'll drive you."

I'm already shaking my head and attempting to give him a bright smile. "Stay here with them and sort out our next plan of action."

Ren stares at me for a long moment before he nods. "Fine." I thank God that Ren's not the smothering type. "I'll walk you out and make sure you get there okay."

My outfit is far from sexy. Too damn bad, Diego. I'm wearing something similar to the last time he saw me. Black yoga pants and this time a hoodie because it's chilly outside. Ren walks me out to his truck and gives me a chaste kiss. I drive slowly over to his house down the street and make a great show of climbing out and waving. He remains from his watch until I disappear onto the porch. I wait a few minutes before peeking around the house. He's gone back inside. With shaky legs, I hurry back to the truck and haul ass out of the neighborhood. It isn't until I'm several miles away with nobody following me that I relax.

I spend the entire half-hour drive to the restaurant worrying. I didn't bring a weapon. I don't have my wallet. I didn't tell anyone where I was going. All I have is my phone shoved into the pocket of my hoodie. When I pull up to the restaurant, I'm happy to see it's bustling with people. Busy is good. Busy means he can't do anything stupid like accost me.

I wait several minutes before climbing out of the truck. My feet carry me inside to the hostess stand. I'm queasy, and the scent of seafood mixed with my nerves makes my stomach roil. I am just about to ask the server for a table when an arm slips around my waist. Before I can let out a scream, warm breath tickles my ear.

"Looking sexy as ever, cariño," Diego murmurs and bites my lobe. "Table for two." The hostess's eyes linger on us for a moment before she waves for us to follow her. I attempt to jerk out of his grip, but he holds me like we're lovers. The moment we reach the booth, he guides me into the seat and slides in beside me. I glare at him and he simply chuckles.

"My wife will have water," he tells the woman. "She's expecting. I'll have a glass of your house wine."

When she leaves, I punch him in his side. "You're such a fucking dick."

"You're the only person I have ever known who is brave enough to not only hit me but also to call me such names." He leans in and kisses my cheek. "I've killed men for much less. But you, my dear sweet kitten, I'm amused by you. If we're being honest, it gets me really fucking hard." His hand grips mine. "Would you like to feel just how hard?"

"I'm going to be sick," I groan, shaking my head.

He laughs and releases me. "Don't be so dramatic, Mrs. Rojas. Where I'm from, most women are actually quite attracted to me."

"I'm not most women."

He reaches across the table and snags a package of

crackers from the basket. After he opens them up, he hands me a cracker.

"So I can see," he says with a chuckle.

With a huff, I accept the cracker and begrudgingly munch on it. He leans on his elbow on the table so he can watch me eat. His lips curve into a pleased smile. Once I've downed the cracker, I meet his stare.

"Why are we here?" I demand.

He hands me another cracker, which I take. "Camilo. The old fuck is really losing his poor mind. Seems that you, cariño, really stirred some shit up."

I suppress a shudder at the very thought of Camilo being angry with me. The man is scary. All the tales of him torturing the people who wronged him replay in my head.

"You need protection, no?"

I snap out of my daze and frown at him. "From you?" I scoff. "I don't think so. I have protection."

He narrows his eyes at me and strokes his goatee with his finger and thumb in a contemplative manner. "Who exactly is your protection detail? Rafe Gonzalez? Your daddy? Because if you recall, they didn't protect you so well the last time we met."

"It doesn't matter," I spit out. "I'm protected."

The asshole leans in and sniffs me like I'm some piece of meat he wants to cook up and eat later. "My men took down your men easily once before. I'm sure it won't be hard for Camilo to do the same. But Camilo Rojas doesn't incapacitate, he kills."

He unwraps another cracker and hands it to me. We're momentarily interrupted when the server comes to our table. Diego blurts out an order and sends her back on her way.

Then, his predatory gaze is back on me.

"What do you want from me?" I ask. "Beside something sexual."

He laughs and stretches his arm across the booth behind me and leans closer. "I want all the information you have in that pretty little head of yours on the Rojas operations. I know you were friends with the little red headed girl. I know you saw how things worked with her father and the shipyard. Then, you were a witness to everything Duvan did. I want the details because I'm going to be running the show very soon."

"You're just going to take it all away from Oscar?" I question with a glare.

He lifts a black eyebrow and smirks. "The boy?"

I almost laugh at him. "When exactly was the last time you saw Oscar? He's far from a boy."

Shrugging, he runs his finger along the outside of my arm. "No matter. I want their territory. You're going to help give it to me. And in exchange, I keep you safe from retaliation."

The very idea of betraying Oscar sickens me. I don't trust Diego one single bit.

"No."

He slaps the table hard enough to make our glasses slosh and me yelp out in surprise. "No is not the answer I was looking for. So far, I have been generous with you, cariño. But you're pushing me right now. You're pissing me off and I'm three seconds from dragging you out of here by your hair and taking you back home with me so I can teach your smart mouth what I do to little girls who misbehave." I let out a whimper when he clutches my thigh to the point of pain.

The woman arrives with the food and Diego flirts with her while I consider his words. Carefully, I unwrap my cloth napkin and set it in my lap. When he's distracted, I slip the knife inside the sleeve of my hoodie. She leaves and he picks up a crab leg. I remain silent as he cracks it open with a crab cracker. Then, he dips a big chunk of meat in some butter sauce before holding it to my lips.

I shake my head and his face darkens.

"Don't make me pry your mouth open in front of all these people because I will. Do as you're told," he hisses.

Suppressing a grumble, I open my mouth and accept the food. He smirks and then pulls off a piece of meat for himself. The entire meal goes on this way. Even though the food is surprisingly good, I'm disgusted by this man. Once he finishes, he wraps his arm around me and hugs me to him. I remain frozen as he pets me as though I'm a small animal. What is it with this guy and petting? He should get a dog.

"I want the information," he says softly, his touch gentle.

"I'll only help you under one condition."

He tenses but releases me. "Go on."

"If I tell you, you can't hurt Oscar."

"Done."

"And I want that protection extended to my friends and family."

He reaches into his pocket and retrieves something. "Of course, cariño. Text me a list. It'll be done."

"Once I tell you what I know, Camilo and Esteban and their people will come after me. I'm pregnant and somewhat happy. I don't want this disrupting my life." Our eyes meet and he nods.

"Anything else?"

"Please don't tell them where you got this information. I know you're an asshole of epic proportions but I'd like to think of you as a business acquaintance. I'll tell you what I know but I'm counting on you to uphold your end of all parts of our deal."

He strokes my cheek with his thumb. "So beautiful. I do a lot of business with men in South America but you've been my most worthy opponent. It would seem I have a soft spot for you." He smirks and slides his thumb over my bottom lip. "I often think of your big round ass when I'm balls deep in one of my wives. Perhaps one day the fantasy will come true."

I start to tell him off but then he dangles something shiny in front of me. My necklace and Duvan's ring.

"You fixed it," I choke out.

He smirks. "Well, I did break it."

At seeing my jewelry, I can't help but burst into tears. He fastens it around my neck and hugs me to him. I don't want to be in his embrace but I feel like I've just made a necessary deal with this devil.

His hand that strokes me in a comforting move slides under my hoodie and up my front. I let out a yelp when his finger strokes my bare belly.

"It would be so easy just to take you home with me," he murmurs against my hair.

The knife hidden in my sleeve slides into my hand and I press the sharp tip against his hard cock that strains against his slacks. He lets out a hiss of shock.

"It would be so easy just to take this," I poke hard enough to make him grunt, "home with me."

His hand retreats from under my shirt and he chuckles. I reluctantly pull the knife away from his junk and glare at him.

"Cariño," he says with a wolfish grin. "Did I ever tell you I like you?"

I roll my eyes and point at his phone. "Too many times. Now take some notes. I have a lot to say."

# XV | Ren

Calder: Luci and I are going to see that new Ryan Reynolds movie. You guys want to come?

Me: Sounds cool. Just ask Brie if she's feeling up to it.

Calder: Ummm. She's probably on YOUR lap. You ask her.

Me: Ha. Seriously, just ask her.

Calder: Duuuude. Do you want me to text her? Wtf.

Me: Stop being a dumbass. She's over there so just ask her.

Calder: Ren, she's not here.

Panic slices through me, and I nearly knock back the kitchen chair I was sitting in to bolt to the front door. As soon as I open the door and look down at my house, my heart nearly explodes.

"She's gone!" I holler over my shoulder to Dad and Gabe.

I've already taken off running down the road to my house. I'm barefoot and not nearly dressed warm enough for the chilly November air but I don't want to lose any time. While

174

on my run, I dial Brie's number. It goes straight to voicemail.

"Fuuuuck!" I yell as I pound up my driveway.

When I sling open the front door, Luciana and Calder look over their shoulders from the couch in confusion.

"She's gone," I breathe out as I hurry to my room to grab a pair of shoes. Snagging a hoodie on the way back out, I bark at Calder. "I need your keys, man. She's gone."

My brother jolts to his feet. "I'm coming with you. Luci, go over to Brie's until I get back."

We both trot back out to his Tahoe and, by this point, Dad and Gabe are in the driveway both looking as panicked as I feel.

"She's not answering. Dad, pull up the location on her phone and text me the address. Gabe, keep trying to call her. I knew something wasn't right when she left in such a hurry," I growl as I climb into the driver's seat.

Gabe hands off a sleeping Toto to Luciana before he and my father take off running back to her house. I don't look back as I peel out of the neighborhood.

"So she's just gone?" Calder questions in confusion.

"Yep," I huff as I gas it down the road.

"Where the fuck are we going?"

"I don't know," I roar and beat my fist on the steering wheel. "Keep calling her but keep an eye out for Dad's call."

I've just merged onto the highway when Dad calls. Calder puts him on speaker.

"Phone records show some texts from an unknown number. Looks like some guy named Diego Gomez." He rattles off the address to a seaside restaurant. Thank fuck I'm already headed in the right direction. "Gabe and I are ten minutes behind you. Don't do anything stupid." I can hear Gabe snarling in the back ground. "Hold on," Dad grunts in annoyance.

"THAT'S THE CRAZY COLOMBIAN CUNT!" Gabe bellows. "She's not fucking safe with him. I'm going to cut his eyeballs out if he so much as looks at her."

I run my fingers through my hair and hit the accelerator. Calder's knuckles turn white as he holds on to the dash. I'm easily going ninety—it'll be a miracle if I don't get pulled over. We weave in and out of traffic as Gabe tells me how dangerous Diego is. And he doesn't even know the half of it. The asshole terrified the hell out of Brie and made promises of brutality. She can't handle someone so ruthless and powerful by herself.

The ride should take at least thirty minutes but Calder and I fly into the parking lot in just under twenty-three. I don't even shut off the ignition before I'm clambering out of the Tahoe and hauling ass into the restaurant.

"Hispanic male. Scary looking. Younger Hispanic woman wearing a grey hoodie," I huff out. "Have you seen them?"

The hostess nods. "Yeah, they just left, actually. Maybe five minutes ago."

I nearly knock Calder over in the doorway but then shove past him back into the parking lot. I see my truck but it's empty. I'm about to go fucking nuts when a black Town Car slowly rolls past. Charging for it, I launch myself on the hood of it to stop it. An old man with a grey beard and an equally old woman stare back at me in horror. The man slams on the brakes and I slide back off the car.

"Over here, crazy!" Calder hollers. "Jesus! You trying to get killed?"

My gaze snaps over to his. Beside him stands my favorite person. And she looks unharmed.

"Fuck, Brie!" I trot over to her and nearly tackle her. With a groan of relief, I wrap my arms around her and crush her against my chest. "What the fuck? You scared the shit out of me!"

She stiffens in my arms. "I had to go."

My palms find her cheeks and I glare at her. "The fuck you did! You just snuck off and met with a man who's known for being a psychopath. Alone! What were you thinking, goddammit?!"

She huffs and tries to push away from me, but I refuse to let her go. "I had to!" Her lips tremble as the fear from meeting with him becomes present. That prick scares her. Hell, he scares me.

"Come here," I growl and smash my lips to hers. She kisses me frantically as if I have the power to erase whatever stressful situation she just encountered. When our lips break apart, she starts to sob.

"I-I didn't think about it. I j-j-just wanted to get my jewelry back," she cries against my chest.

I squeeze her tight and kiss the top of her head. "We do this shit together, Brie. Please. You've got two babies you need to protect. You can't do that alone. You've got to stop trying to fix all of these problems by yourself. I'm here. Let me be here for you."

She nods. "I'm sorry, Ren. I'm so sorry."

I'm stroking her hair and assuring her everything will be okay when another car flies into the lot. Seconds later, Gabe jerks her from my grip.

"What the fuck, Brie baby?" he snaps but squeezes her tight enough that I'm afraid he'll crush her. "I'm going to kill that motherfucker! Where the hell is he?"

She pushes away from her father and launches herself back into my arms. "He's gone. I made a deal with him."

Dad gives me a wide-eyed stare while Gabe kicks the gravel under his feet.

"We don't make deals with that fucker," Gabe snaps.

I squeeze her to me and level him with a *calm-the-fuck-down* stare. "Let her talk."

She sniffles and lets out a sigh. "He wanted to know every detail of the Rojas operations. I told him because he promised me protection. He promised protection to all of you."

Gabe grips at his hair and shakes his head. "Oh, sweet girl," he growls. "And you believed him?"

Her chin tilts up and she looks at me. Uncertainty flickers in her brown eyes. "I trusted him to do the right thing. I honestly don't have a choice. Camilo is pissed. He wants to get me back for selling off Duvan's assets. That old man is scary. The things he's done to people for far less..." She shudders and buries her face against my chest.

"This was stupid—" Gabe starts but I cut him off.

"Enough," I snap. "She did what she thought she needed to do. You and Dad keep digging into the cartels. I don't trust them at all. Not even Oscar. So find out what they're up to. Let's stay ahead of this." Looking down at Brie, I kiss her nose. "And you," I murmur. "Please don't do that ever again. You scared the shit out of all of us. Promise me, baby."

She nods. "He scares me so bad." Her body trembles again as if the thought of him simply terrifies her.

"I want a gun," I bite out to Gabe. If anyone can get me illegal and untraceable shit, it would be him. "For all of us. Luciana. Calder. Me and Brie. I'm not going to feel settled until we all have a way to protect ourselves."

Gabe is already storming back to Dad's vehicle but he's nodding. Dad grips my shoulder and gives me a firm stare. "I'm going to find out where they're holing up. If I have to leak the info to the Feds, I will. We're going to get rid of this threat," he assures me before stalking off after Gabe.

Calder holds his hand out for his keys. "Drive the speed limit on the way home, you crazy freak. I'd really like to go to that movie later and I can't do that if you and Brie are splattered all over the highway."

I chuckle and toss his keys at him. Once he's gone, I guide Brie over to my truck. I open her door for her. She shakily sits down inside. By the time I'm inside with her, she's somber and quiet but much calmer than before.

"Are you okay?" I question.

She swallows and nods. "I just hate when he touches me." Then a beat of silence. "It reminds me of him. Esteban." Her body shudders. "I can't ever go through something like that again."

Rage blooms in my chest, and I fist my hands. If that prick were here, I'd bash his head in. "He better not ever touch you. As long as I have anything to do with it, he won't."

Her lips tug into a half smile as she relinquishes my keys. "You're cute when you're protective."

Smirking, I shrug my shoulders and start the truck. "Must mean I'm cute all the time."

It's been nearly a month since Brie gave us the disappearing act scare. We've all been on high alert, but I have to say, sleeping with a gun under my pillow each night certainly helps. Brie is always on edge, and I hate that she has to live her life that way.

"I can't deal if she's going to be there," Brie murmurs as we walk hand in hand to my house. I can see Mom and Dad's car in the driveway next to Calder's. No trace of Gabe and Hannah, thank God.

"Dad already asked them not to come. I think Toto will be there, though," I tell her.

She doesn't pull a face at the mention of her sister. "I thought your dad was a vegan."

"He is. Calder told him he could eat vegetables but we were having turkey on Thanksgiving for once," I say with a chuckle.

Brie laughs. "I actually like your parents. Do you you think this is hard on them? Especially your mom?"

I let out a breath of air. "Yeah. Gabe is the villain in her eyes. He's the villain in mine too. But he's also your dad and the father of my adorable niece. It's complicated, but I think we're doing better than most families with this much baggage."

She stops when we get to the front porch. I can hear voices inside and can smell food already.

"I can't imagine my daddy doing those terrible things to Baylee. My heart begs me not to believe her, but I saw the look in her eyes. I've seen that same terrified look in my own eyes in the mirror whenever I think about Esteban and what he did to me. Why would he hurt her?" she questions, her chin quivering.

I stroke her bangs from her face and kiss her forehead. "I don't know, babe. I don't know. But Mom has always kind of been a badass. And I can kick your dad's ass if I need to. He's not hurting anyone else in this family ever again."

"Do you think he's hurt other women?"

I think about all the stories Dad told me recently about their past. Gabe was more than a villain. He was psychopathic and predatory. Dad told me about the other women he "trained." Something tells me that Brie doesn't need the image of her dad tarnished further. She has enough going on in her head right now.

"I'm not sure," I lie. "But all that matters now is that he's trying to be a better person. He's good to my sister, even though she doesn't deserve it. And he loves you and Toto with everything he has. I'm not saying he's a good man," I tell her with a sigh. "But I'm not saying he's completely bad either. He's still your dad no matter what he's done or no matter what he will do."

She nods and lifts her chin. "Thank you."

Smirking, I nuzzle her nose with mine. "For what? For this morning? I can still taste your sweet cunt on my lips."

A squeal erupts from her and she shoves me, but a grin turns her full lips up. "No, punk. Thank you for being my friend. I mean, you're more than a friend because we practically live together, but you know what I mean. Thank you for being a friend *and* a lover. Thank you for being you."

I snag her wrist and haul her into my arms. Twisting her so her back is flush against my chest, I splay both palms on her much fuller stomach. Next week, we get to find out the sex. "One day I'm going to be more than just a friendly lover," I murmur against her hair. "One day I'm going to be so much more, Momma."

She relaxes against me, and I kiss her neck. The front

door opens and Calder steps out with his hands on his hips. He's not wearing a shirt, no surprise there, but he's wearing a stupid apron that says "Kiss the Cook" on it.

"Everyone's waiting to eat while you guys practically fuck on the front porch," he chides. "Seriously. If my mashed potatoes get cold, so help me, I'm going to kick your ass."

Brie laughs and pulls away from my grip. She gives Calder a kiss on the cheek before going inside.

"You're more of a woman than Martha Stewart is," I tell him with a smirk.

"Laugh it up now, fucker," he grumbles. "You won't be laughing when you come in your pants after you taste those mashed potatoes."

"Make your own gravy?" I taunt to get a reaction out of him.

When he gags, I snort with laughter.

The punch to my gut was worth the look of pure horror on his face.

# XVI | Brie

A BOY AND A GIRL.

I'm still in shock. Two healthy little babies according to the sonogram. The moment was bittersweet. Duvan wasn't there to share it with me but Ren was. And despite not being the father, he was thrilled.

"Any word from Oscar?" Ren questions from the doorway of what will be the nursery. We've still yet to decorate it. The only thing I've bought so far is a glider. Sometimes, I sit in here for hours. Especially when Ren is distracted with his online courses. It relaxes me. In a way, I feel closer to Duvan in these quiet moments while I absently stroke his ring, which hangs at the base of my throat. Just his memory, our babies, and the quietness. During those times, we're the family that we'll never truly get to be.

"Not in a month," I tell him with a sigh before turning my attention to him. Big mistake. He's just gotten out of the shower after a workout over at his house. The white towel hangs dangerously low on his tapered hips revealing a delicious V and a happy trail of hair that leads right to his impressive cock. Said cock, although flaccid at the moment, can be seen bulging from behind the towel. The doctor warned me my hormones would be off the charts. And lately, now that my morning sickness has gone away for the most part, I find myself physically craving Ren's cock inside of me. A lot.

He saunters into the room past me and looks out the window. The window in the babies' room faces the ocean. When it's warmer, I'll be able to open it and hear the waves crashing.

"Do you think Vee is okay?" he questions. His shoulders are tense and it squashes all of my sexual thoughts as reality rushes back in.

"I don't know. I'm worried about her. She's just gone. Oscar filed a police report ages ago. Of course the cops have no leads. Has your dad found out anything else?" I ask as I stand and make my way over to him. His back tattoo is completely finished now. Every time I see it, I want to cry. The tree is big and strong and takes up most of his back. But it's what's under the tree that steals my heart. A fierce tigress with a no-nonsense gleam in her eyes. Curled up in front of her are two baby cubs. I don't have to ask him to know that he's the tree. And truth be told, I see him as the tree in my life. Steady. Unyielding. Protective from the harsh storms that always seem to whip my way from every direction. The fact that he cares for all of me, including my little cubs, has my heart stammering in my chest. His love is too much sometimes. I feel undeserving of it.

"Dad will find something. I'm sure of it," he says softly.

He relaxes once I wrap my arms around his solid middle. My cheek presses against his colorful back and I let out a sigh. His palms cover mine on my lower stomach and we remain silent for a bit.

"What if she's dead?" A choked sob escapes me.

Ren turns in my arms and hugs me to him. "Shhh," he murmurs. "Don't talk like that."

Tears roll out, and I once again curse myself for all of these stupid emotions swirling around me twenty-four-seven. Vee is tough but she's also sheltered. I'm afraid if something bad happened to her, she wouldn't be able to cope.

"Calder was making lasagna when I left. Wanted to know if we were coming for dinner. Luciana misses you," he tells me, changing the subject.

I yawn and shrug my shoulders. "We can go but I'm so tired. I hate that I'm sleepy all the time."

He chuckles and kisses my forehead. "How about you just relax? I'll go grab us a plate in a bit and bring it back. Luciana can come visit tomorrow."

I give him a wicked grin as I tug at his towel. "Maybe you should tuck me into bed first."

Before the towel even hits the floor, he scoops me into his arms and charges back to my room—I say it's *my* room, but he's practically moved all of his clothes into the closet and drawers. I'd be lying if I said I didn't like his crap all over the place, mingled with mine. It feels homey and comfortable having him here all the time.

He strides into the room and sets me on the bed. All I have on is one of his T-shirts and a pair of panties. Both get torn from me in a matter of seconds. Before I can utter another word, he climbs on top of me and is inside of me before my next breath.

Sex with Ren is fulfilling and exciting.

But the part I crave the most from it is that I can feel his love pouring from him like a never ending fountain. I drink greedily from it. I try to reciprocate the best I can but I'm not as good at it. He makes it seem like loving me is as easy as breathing.

"We won't get as many of these moments when our babies get here," he murmurs against my throat as he thrusts into me. "Gotta steal them while we can."

I freeze at his words.

Our babies.

I'm hit by a thousand emotions at once. Joy. Fury. Happiness. Anger. Despair and sadness. Excitement. Dread.

"Oh, fuck," he grunts and slows to a stop. He lifts up to give me a pained expression. Dark hair that's growing longer hangs down past his eyebrows into his eyes. His full lips are parted as he attempts to find the right words to say.

He becomes a blur as emotion overcomes me. I want to tell him I'm glad he wants to take care of the three of us. I want to explain to him that despite this being a sad time for me, he makes me happy. But none of those things come out. Instead, words I don't mean trickle out. They taste dirty and wrong on my tongue.

"They're *my* babies," I choke out. "Me and Duvan's babies."

The look of heartbreak on his face makes it feel as though someone is cracking open my chest. He's inside of me with a look of frustration and horror painted on his face. Neither of us move. Both of us are confused about how we're supposed to feel.

"Brie," he murmurs and buries his face against my neck. His thick cock pushes deeper inside of me at the action causing me to gasp. "I'm sorry. I just can't help but feel possessive over every part of you. You know I love you. I love them too."

I sob as I clutch his hair. Rocking against him, I urge him to continue fucking me despite the raging storm of emotions whipping around inside me.

"I won't feel guilty for loving you or them," he bites out, the fierceness something I can feel cutting permanent grooves in my heart. "Not ever."

His words are like an accelerant on my impending orgasm. My body shudders as I lose myself to the pleasure. All conflicting emotions fly out of me as I allow myself one moment of undiluted bliss. He bucks into me a few more times before his own heat surges into me. When he finishes, we remain tangled up in silence. After some time, he kisses my throat and pulls out of me.

"I'm going to go get us some food," he says in a husky voice, his gaze not meeting mine. "Try and get some rest." His back muscles ripple as he yanks clothes on—the inked tree moving but still unbreakable. He's angry at me. Deservedly so. Hell, I'm angry at me. Sometimes my emotions are confusing but how I feel about Ren is unwavering. So why did I say something to hurt him? Truth is…I don't know. I wish I were brave enough to climb out of the bed after him and beg him to understand the conflicting slew of emotions wreaking havoc inside of me. The way he's tearing my heart right from my chest and keeping it as his own. He casts one more troubled look at me that makes my heart rate quicken. The flash of anger in his eyes unsettles me.

*I want to be yours, Ren.*

*I want them to be yours.*

But the words don't fall from my mouth like I want them to and my bottom lip does nothing but tremble as I watch him walk right out the door.

I clench my eyes closed and will the ache in my chest to subside. When he gets back, I'll explain to him. I'll let him know that he's everything to me. That sometimes I say things I don't mean because the guilt inside of me is a curse I can't escape.

I wasn't supposed to be happy.

But I am.

Because of Ren.

So why is it so hard admitting that out loud?

I wake to my phone buzzing on the nightstand. One look at the clock tells me I've only just fallen asleep. That Ren hasn't been gone more than five minutes.

**Ozzy: I found her. She's in bad shape. I need your help.**

I blink away my sleep as I sit up.

**Me: Where? What happened?**

**Ozzy: I'm at your front door. Come now. We don't have time to waste.**

I jolt into action and throw on some yoga pants. Then, I find one of Ren's hoodies that smells like him to throw on over my T-shirt. I stuff my feet into a pair of Uggs and grab my phone before hurrying downstairs. When I sling the door open, Ozzy stands there looking horrible.

His eyes have dark circles under them and his hair is even longer than the last time I saw him. He's an utter wreck. As soon as he sees me, he grabs my elbow.

"Hurry," he snaps.

I put on the brakes and shake my head. "I need to call

Ren."

He rolls his eyes and releases me. "Fine. Do it in the car. Tell him to meet us at her parents' house."

We both climb into Oscar's car and I dial Ren. He doesn't answer, so I leave him a voicemail telling him Ozzy found Vee and that we're headed to her parents' now. I shove the phone back into the pocket of my hoodie and regard my friend. He looks nothing like the boy I remember.

He's a lost, broken man.

"Are you okay?" I question and reach for his hand.

"Peachy," he snaps and jerks his hand away. "Really. What do *you* think, Brie?"

Tears prickle at my eyes, but I refuse to cry in front of him. He's upset so I'll allow him to be an ass. Under normal circumstances, I'd be telling him where to stick his attitude. But he managed to find Vee and it sounds bad. If there was ever a time for allowances, the time is now.

Oscar drives easily fifteen miles over the speed limit the entire way there. I'm so lost in thought that I don't even realize we're heading in the opposite direction of her parents' house, until we're pulling into Heath's shipyard.

"Wait," I say, sitting up and pointing through the glass. "I thought you said we were going to their house."

He gives me a noncommittal shrug as he parks the car and climbs out. I scramble out after him, suddenly wishing I would have spoken to Ren before I left in such a hurry.

"This way," he tells me over his shoulder as he stalks toward the gate that leads to all the shipping containers.

"Hold on," I blurt as I dial Ren again. It rings and rings until it goes to voicemail again. I'm about to leave a message when my phone gets torn from my hand. Oscar's face is positively murderous as he heaves it as far as he can throw it. I gape at him in shock for a long second before I begin to process what just happened.

This was a trick.

Vee isn't here.

But I can bet my entire bank account that his crazy father is.

"Shit," I hiss as I back away from him.

He lets out a growl as he charges after me. Oscar is bigger and stronger than me. So when he grabs my elbow, he's easily able to drag me behind him despite my fighting him off. Someone opens the gates, and I yell out to them. The howl of the biting wind seems to carry my voice away, right along with the sunlight. It's dark and grey and dreary…much like what awaits me.

"Help!" I swat at Ozzy. "Let me go!"

He ignores me as he storms along at a breakneck speed. My tears fall freely now. I don't know what's about to happen but every nerve ending in my body promises that it won't be good. I'm dragged through a maze of containers that are stacked on top of each other until he stops in front of one. The door is ajar. Panic immobilizes me as I imagine what sort of horrors wait for me on the other side. When he has trouble getting me to follow, he hooks his arm just under my breasts and lifts me. I kick and scream to no avail.

The moment we enter the container, a foul stench wafts around me and makes me gag. Oscar hands me off to two larger men who easily wrangle me into a chair. I scream at them to let me go but, within minutes, they have me tied to the chair. Oscar delivers the blow of betrayal when he slaps a strip of duct tape over my mouth.

It's dark inside the container aside from the grey light streaming in from the doorway. I frantically look around to see what I'm up against. There's movement and sound coming from the dark part of the metal cage but I can't see what it is.

Realization hits me like a cold splash of water.

I'm going to die in here.

Both my babies and I are never leaving this box.

As hot tears race down my cheeks, the only thing I can think of is Ren. How as soon as he realizes I'm gone, he'll go mad trying to find me. A sob fights for escape in my throat but the tape keeps it locked away.

"If it isn't the little puta who keeps screwing over my sons," a familiar, heavily accented voice snarls. Camilo. All three of Camilo's sons look a lot like him, but not one, not even Esteban, have that sick gleam in their eyes. Eyes that point to an evil past. And an empty soul. A shudder wracks through me the moment he comes into view. Blood soaks the front of his white dress shirt and a look of rage is painted on his normally cool features. I tremble and shake my head at him pleading for him to not do whatever it is he has planned.

"First, you get my middle son killed because of your precious little bollo," he bites out, gesturing between my legs. "My own business partner betrayed me because he wanted it so bad." He comes to stand right in front of me. "Débiles. Weak." With the toe of his dress shoe, he pokes at me between my spread legs and regards me as if I'm vermin. "What exactly is so special about it? Is it lined with cocaína? What makes grown men estúpido over your whore snatch?"

I shake and attempt to free myself from the restraints.

"¿Dónde está mi cuchillo?" he snaps over his shoulder.

My cries become too much with the tape over my mouth and I start to hyperventilate. I frantically look for Oscar in the shadows, but he's nowhere to be found. When Camilo kneels in front of me, I meet his hate-filled gaze. I close my eyes, though, the moment I see the knife in his grip.

God, please no.

A ripping of fabric has my heart beating right out of my chest. Thankfully, aside from a quick bite or two from the knife against my flesh, he leaves me otherwise unharmed. Naked from the waist down but alive.

"Mírame," he growls. "Look at me."

I'm shaking badly but I open my eyes to meet his gaze. With the tip of the knife, he pokes at the lips of my pussy. Not hard enough to break the skin, but hard enough to scare the crap out of me.

"My wife's snatch was better looking," he observes. "What makes yours so special? I mean, my eldest son broke the rules of our family to fuck it. Went against our code to put his dick inside of you. And we all know how goddamned distraught Oscar was when he found out he wasn't winning *this* prize." He pokes me again. "Me das asco."

I shake my head and plead with him. He wants answers but he won't let me even speak. A scream resounds from behind the tape the moment he touches me with his pudgy fingers. They prod at me. Tug at my pubic hair. And then, to my horror, enter me. Bile threatens to rise up my throat but being that I have tape over my mouth, I decide I'll do whatever it takes to keep it down.

Closing my eyes, I think of Ren. I think of the way he proudly called these precious babies ours. I'd give anything to rewind a couple of hours and agree that we're his family now. That I want him to take care of us.

That I love him too.

The realization of that fact has me sobbing harder than before. Camilo fingers me almost painfully, but it's better if I disconnect my mind from the physical act.

Ren. Ren. Ren.

God, I miss him.

If he were here, he'd protect me.

"That's enough, Papá," Oscar snarls from the shadows.

I pop my eyes open to see Camilo glaring in the direction he's in. "Son, I must be honest," Camilo says with a cold laugh as he pulls his fingers from within me. "I don't see what's so fucking special about her cunt. But clearly, you see it. It's a goddamned cunt del otro mundo." He sniffs his fingers and I gag. This seems to anger him though because with a quick, hard swing, he cracks his knuckles across my cheek.

Stars blind my vision for a moment.

"You like that, puta?" He raises his hand like he's going to hit me again but he never strikes.

Oscar emerges from the darkness and glowers at his father. "She's pregnant. That's enough."

Camilo stands, no longer interested in hitting me, and faces off with his son. "Hijo, we talked about this. She's going to pay for what she's done to our family."

Oscar's gaze meets mine, and I see a flash of regret in his eyes. I plead with mine for him to help me. With reluctance, he drags them away to glare back at his father.

"If you have such a problem with my methods, then *you*

exact our revenge," Camilo barks. "Did you want to fuck her magical pussy once more? By all means, get your rocks off, hijo. The boys and I will leave if that will make you feel better. Rafe, though, stays."

My eyes dart into the darkness. If Rafe is here, maybe he'll help me.

"Fine," Oscar bites out. "Just go."

"If I don't hear the puta screaming in fifteen minutes, I'm coming back to finish the job," Camilo warns. "Esto es tu deber."

His son gives him a clipped nod. Camilo and several other men file out. They shut the doors, leaving us in pitch-black darkness. All that can be heard are my whimpers.

"Why?" Oscar chokes out after several moments. "Why did you fuck everything up?"

When I don't answer, he walks closer to me. I can sense his presence within touching distance. His breath is ragged, and for the first time, I smell liquor on it. Warm hands clutch my thighs, and I hear his knees bang on the metal as he falls in front of me. I wriggle in my bindings, praying I can get loose.

"If things went differently, you'd be pregnant with *my* baby," he utters, his words nostalgic almost.

I whimper when his thumbs rub circles on my inner thighs.

"I lost my chance with you. A chance to make my father proud. Then, I lost her. A chance at something else…something good. But both chances were stolen from me. I can't fucking win," he snips out in a disgusted tone.

His head falls against my breasts, and I can really smell the alcohol on him.

"I don't know how to fix this," he admits, his voice ragged with emotion. "I don't want you to die."

When he reaches up and tears the tape from my mouth, I let out the long sob I'd been holding in.

"P-P-Please, Ozzy. Don't let him hurt me. I'm pregnant with twins. Your brother's babies. Don't let them die. Please. You c-can help me. We can get out of this. P-Please," I plead through my tears.

"Shhh," he groans before his mouth presses against mine in a sloppy drunk kiss. "Shhh." His hands roam my body clumsily. "This is all so fucked up."

"Just untie me," I plead. "We c-can fix it." My teeth chatter as the terror of my situation completely consumes me.

"My father is right," he says in a husky tone. "There's something about you that we can't ignore." His fingers, much gentler than his father's, prod at my opening. "For so long I wanted to fuck you, Brie."

"Well, you can't," I bite out, squirming against his unwanted touch. "I'm not yours. But you can do right by your brother and get me out of here. I'm pregnant with two babies. Your brother's babies. Snap the hell out of whatever it is you're going through, Ozzy. You're no better than Esteban."

My words have him jerking away from me. I can't see him in the dark but I can hear him pacing on the metal floor.

"I'm not like him," he snaps.

"No and you're not like your father either," I try, my tone gentler. "You're like Duvan. You're good. Please come back to me. I need my friend right now...not this...not this monster your father wants you to be."

Someone beats on the doors and yells, "Ten more minutes."

This seems to jolt Oscar into action. A flashlight comes on and he points it in my face. I squint against it as he starts untying me. Relief floods through me until he jerks me to my feet. He drops the flashlight with a clang and it points into the darkened part of the container from earlier. I let out a scream when I see Rafe tied to a chair in the corner. His eyes have been cut from their sockets and his intestines hang out of his stomach.

"Noooooo," I shriek as I fight against Oscar.

He grunts as he drags me over to a dirty mattress in the corner. I'm tossed on my ass. Before I can even move, he's pinning me to the filthy makeshift bed.

"This will only take ten minutes," he assures me loud enough to make the container echo with his words. "Now hold fucking still. It's my turn."

# XVII | Ren

I DROP THE KEYS ON THE ISLAND IN THE KITCHEN AND PUT the lasagna in the refrigerator. Chances are, she's passed out so I won't wake her to eat. While over at my house, I tried not to obsess over her crushing words.

*They're my babies. Me and Duvan's babies.*

Those words, spoken so vehemently, rocked me to my core. It reminded me that no matter how much time passes, no matter how many times I love her with my body, that we're never really any further than we were when we started. I ache knowing she'll never love me like she loved him.

And yet…

I don't give up. She's mine. Even though she said she couldn't love me, she did promise me that. That she belonged to me. In my head, they're one in the same. One day she'll let down her guard just a little and I'll be there to swoop her into my arms. I won't ever give up on her. If we go round and round until our deaths, so be it. At least I'll have her. At least I can love her with everything I have. I don't need it back. I just need her.

I tiptoe up the stairs, careful not to wake her. Before heading into her bedroom, I stop off in the nursery. We still have so much to do before the babies get here. I'm scratching my jaw, figuring out if two cribs will fit along one wall when I remember I bought an app the other day for this purpose. It allows you to measure walls. When I reach into my pocket, I remember I left my phone charging on my nightstand in Brie's room.

I'm still mulling over our conversation from earlier when I walk into our room. The first thing I notice is the utter silence. She's not in bed.

"Babe?" I call out and storm into the bathroom. When I find it empty too, my heart rate starts thundering. "Babe!" I stomp into the bedroom and yank my phone from the charger.

Two missed calls from Brie.

Fuck!

I start listening as I clomp down the stairs two at a time. In the first message, she tells me Oscar showed up and they found Vee. That they're going to Vee's parents' house. I snag my keys from the island and break into a sprint out to my truck as I listen to the next message. She curses. Then I hear a crunching sound. And finally...shrieks to let her go that sound far off.

I'm stunned frozen until reality hits me. He fucking took her. Oscar fucking took my girlfriend and is taking her straight to Camilo. Turning on my heel, I run back in the house to collect the gun Gabe gave me and call Dad along the way.

When he answers, I bark out orders. "Find the location

of Brie's phone and then send Gabe. They fucking took her!"

It took Dad fifteen minutes to hack in and find the last ping of her cell phone. As soon as he gave me the location of the shipyard, I hauled ass there. I should wait for Gabe who I know will come ready to slaughter the entire lot of them, but I don't. All I can think about is the fact that they have my pregnant girlfriend. Crazy, evil, psychotic men have my Brie.

Fuck!

As soon as the shipyard comes into view, I pull off alongside the dirt road. I launch out of the truck with my gun locked and loaded. I'm ready to blow the head off of any motherfucker who stands in my way. I should sneak up on them or something, but it's hard to do when time is of the essence. Quickly, I prowl down the road hunched over until I reach an open gate. Once inside, I see several vehicles parked in front of what looks like an office. Another gate stands open that leads straight to where the shipping containers are stacked at least ten high. I'm slinking along the outside, hoping to sneak in when I hear a blood-curdling scream from somewhere inside one of the containers. The scream came from Brie—I would recognize the sound of her voice anywhere.

"Brie!!" I yell, no longer worried about my cover. I charge forward but before I make it very far, something cracks me over the head. Stumbling, I attempt to blink away the blurriness in my vision when another blow hits my skull from behind.

Blackness steals away my sight and consciousness. And

the last thing I hear until I completely fade away are her screams.

"Wake up, asshole."

Pain slices through my head as I attempt to shake away the buzzing in my skull. I'm in a dark room of sorts. The only light that shines through is from a door. Once I blink a few times, I realize I'm in a shipping container.

"You must be the little boyfriend." An old man laughs. It's cold and harsh. "The lawn boy, I presume. You're the little cunt who was fucking my boy's wife on the side?"

I shake my head in a daze. "I don't know what you're talking about."

He swings his fist and it connects with my jaw. My teeth bite down on my bottom lip from the impact and metallic blood gushes into my mouth.

"Don't lie to me. Are you or aren't you the cunt who the little girl was in love with before my son married her?" he snarls.

I go to rub at my jaw but realize through my haze that I'm bound to a chair I'm sitting on. "I never touched her while they were married," I grit out as I spit some blood from my mouth.

The old man comes into the light and squats in front of me. "She's not talking. My youngest boy has been in there with her trying to extract information from her. You see," he says and scratches at his white beard. "Your puta girlfriend sold my son's territory to our motherfucking enemy.

Territory that's been in our family for decades. It wasn't hers to give away. Now she not only pays with her magical cunt but also with her life."

"WHERE THE FUCK IS SHE?" I roar and struggle against the ropes.

He smirks and pats my knee. "My boy Oscar is getting his fill of her pussy before I get her back. I promise you, I'm going to extract the debt from her one square inch of her flesh at a time."

"She's pregnant," I snap. "With your son's babies."

He's silent for a moment.

"Twins, huh?" The old fuck simply shrugs his shoulders. "Presumed. But as far as I know, they're yours."

I spit at him. "What if they're Esteban's?" It's a lie but I don't want him thinking the babies are mine because then he'll have no reason to keep her alive.

Camilo puffs out his chest and fists his hand. "Esteban is disowned. He abandoned our family in our time of need."

"The doctor said they were Duvan's," I try again. "You'd kill your own grandchildren?"

He stands and paces. I hope my words get to him. "I suppose I could keep her around. As a fuck toy for my youngest son until the babies are born. Then, I'll kill her. Smart thinking, lawn boy."

I'm about to go off on him when we hear a struggle outside the container. Then four loud pops of a gun. Camilo runs out the door. A few minutes later, he returns dragging Gabe in by his hair.

Fuck!

"And who the fuck are you?" Camilo demands as he shoves Gabe to the floor. Gabe scrambles back up to his feet and wipes blood off his chin. Camilo aims a hand gun at his face. "I asked who the fuck you are."

Gabe growls. "Your worst motherfuckin' nightmare."

At this, Camilo laughs. "Bind him," he orders to two of his men, who are in the container with us. "This day just keeps getting better and better."

Gabe puts up one helluva fight and ends up head-butting one of the men. But between Camilo and the still-standing man, they wrestle him into submission.

"Where the fuck is Pedro?" Camilo demands, his chest heaving. "This is his shit to deal with."

The man who's not sprawled out unconscious on the floor shakes his head. "This fucker took out four of ours before I tackled him."

Camilo glares at Gabe before turning back to the man. "As in incapacitated or—"

"He blew their heads off."

With a rage-filled roar, Camilo punches Gabe in the stomach hard enough to have him gasping for air.

"Where's Brie?" I demand, hoping to distract them.

"I already told you. Getting her brains fucked out by my son. While he gets what he so desperately wants, I'm going to enjoy myself." He unsheathes a knife from his belt. "Starting with you."

Gabe grunts and struggles from the chair beside me as Camilo slowly prowls toward me. The blade of his knife points right at me as a taunt.

"People who fuck with the Rojas family eventually meet my blade," he seethes. He punches me hard in the gut. Searing pain explodes from the impact. It takes only a second to realize he didn't punch me. He fucking stabbed me.

"J-Just let her go," I choke out. The pain in my stomach steals my breath.

He laughs again. It's cold and ugly. Slowly, he pulls his blade from my middle. I hiss when blood rushes from the gaping hole.

"If you want to fucking slaughter someone, I'm right here," Gabe bellows and struggles against his restraints. "Right the fuck here. Man to old fucking man. Cut me loose and see just how many jabs you can get on *this* man."

Pain throbs from my stomach, and I struggle for air. Camilo looks over at Gabe and smirks. "I would gut you in a heartbeat."

"Wanna fucking bet?" Gabe snarls.

Camilo shakes his head and storms back over to me. He grabs a handful of my hair and jerks my head up. "You don't want this boy to die. Is he yours? Better yet is *she* yours?"

Gabe utters out a *fuck you.*

My eyes keep rolling back in my head, but I fight desperately to keep them open.

"You must be the evil fuck who sent her off to live with Heath. Did you know he was a twisted man? Did you know he wanted to fuck your sweet little girl even back when she was just fifteen years old? She resembles you now that I'm really looking at you." Camilo shrugs and slashes his arm out in front of me. Fire skates across my chest, and I gape down at the slice across my pectoral muscles.

"JUST FUCKING STOP!" Gabe roars.

Camilo wipes his blade against the thigh of his slacks. "I won't stop until I drain the life out of both of you."

"Ren," Gabe snaps, making me jolt with sudden awareness. "Fucking stay with me."

I blink again and attempt to struggle against the ropes. But I'm weak. So damn weak.

"Where was I?" Camilo questions as if we were discussing a football game or some shit. "Oh," he says with a wicked grin that reveals his teeth. "I remember. I was gutting this little piggy."

Pain explodes in my thigh this time as he plunges the knife deep into the muscle. My dizziness evaporates as I scream. Fire lashes at the entry point. I'm feeling overwhelming pain from so many places that I'm starting to lose touch with reality.

Brie.

I close my eyes and envision her sad eyes. Eyes that on occasion twinkle with happiness. I live for those small moments with her. Moments that are worth all the other hard times. Her smiles are like heaven. She's my angel.

"REN!"

I blink my eyes open to Gabe's voice. Turning my head, I manage to see him going fucking crazy in his chair. The man behind him simply laughs. My gaze fixates on the way Gabe loosens his binds around one wrist without our captors even noticing.

"I-I-I love her," I tell my beautiful girl's father. Not that he cares. Not that it matters. I just want it to be heard. The darkness keeps creeping up on me and if it steals me away, I want those words to be the last ones on my lips. "I l-love Brie. I l-l-love the b-babies."

Camilo kneels in front of me. "Cue the fucking tears. We have us a modern day Romeo here." He hollers as if she can hear him wherever she is. "Juliet! Juliet! Your Romeo's heart is bleeding for you."

"J-Just let her go," I murmur. I'm not even sure if the words actually make it outside my mouth.

My eyes fall closed and my head flops forward. The only pain I feel right now is in my heart. Sadness and loss. I don't want to lose her. I finally fucking got her back. Duvan died and it was up to me to be there for her. To see it to the end with her. We were going to be a family. As fucked up as it was, a family.

I think about the first time I made love to her. What feels like eons ago when we were so innocent. Just the two of us under the moonlight by the ocean. Our bodies meeting for the first time in an intimate way.

God, I fucking love her.

Gabe shouts over and over again. I can feel bites and licks of pain but they don't matter anymore. All that matters are her pretty browns staring at me. The way her lips press against mine in the middle of the night. At one time I'd craved having her in the light. But now I want her to find me in this dark.

*Find me, Brie.*

*Fucking find me.*

Black swarms in like a cloud of a million bees.

It shadows my world.

Blinds me.

I can't see her anymore.

*Fucking find me, Brie.*

# XVIII Brie

I BRACE FOR OZZY TO ENTER ME AGAINST MY WILL. My friend. Someone who I thought I loved is about to betray me in the worst possible way. In some ways, this will be worse than it was with Esteban. With Ozzy, I care.

But he doesn't.

I'm jolted to reality when he whispers against the shell of my ear. "They think I'm raping you. We don't have much time. Just scream and make it sound like you're struggling while I figure out what the hell we're going to do."

I gape up at him in the darkness. The small beam of light from the flashlight isn't enough for me to see his face. I'd like to imagine that if I could see him, he'd have the same mischievous expression I remember from before.

He climbs off of me and rises to his feet. Then, he grabs hold of my shoulders and helps me to my feet as well. I'm still wearing Ren's hoodie, so it thankfully covers my ass as it hits about mid thigh and I still have my Uggs on.

"Scream," he hisses as I hear the click of his weapon.

I let out an ear-piercing scream that muffles our footsteps toward the door. With his gun poised and ready to shoot, he slowly drags open the door a crack and peeks outside.

"There's no one out here," he mutters, his voice sounding confused. He drags the door the rest of the way open and we both wince at the screeching sound it makes. Then, he motions for me to follow him. Sunlight is still not visible as a winter storm begins to roll in. The wind is cold and powerful.

"This way," he tells me and motions for me to follow.

I run after him but then stumble to a halt when we come across a dead body. A man who has a bullet through his skull. I can't help but have a surge of hope welling inside me. Maybe Ren was able to find me.

We're headed toward the gate when I hear a familiar voice.

"Daddy?" I murmur.

"We need to go," Oscar hisses and jerks at my arm.

I wriggle from his grasp. "No! My dad is here! I hear him over there!" Pointing, I begin running toward the sound. Oscar curses behind me but quickly passes me with his gun raised. We pass three more unmoving bodies, and I can't help but pray they're all dead. Grunts and cursing and shouting can be heard from a shipping container fifty feet or so ahead that has its door open. When I hear Daddy's horrified voice shouting Ren's name, all thought vanishes from my brain— except for reaching them—as I bolt ahead of Oscar.

As soon as I burst through the door, my entire world tilts on its axis. Blood. So much blood. Like Mom. Like Duvan. It causes me to stumble over my feet and gag from the sight of it. My eyes fixate on my dad for one second. He's bloody and furious, but alive. Ren on the other hand…

"What have you done?" I hiss at Camilo, no longer concerned about my own safety. "WHAT HAVE YOU DONE?"

One of his men appears from the shadows and grabs me from behind. I go crazy trying to escape. He's stronger and slaps a hand over my mouth to keep me quiet. My eyes land on Ren. Sweet, sexy, beautiful, perfect Ren. Completely drenched in blood. His head hangs in front of him and his hair hides his eyes from me. I can't tell if he's still alive or not. A sob catches in my throat as hot tears streak down my cheeks.

"I should have known my son wouldn't have been able to manage you. You probably sweet talked him right out of that container," Camilo says in disgust as he stalks over to Ren. His bloody knife is the only thing I see, though. It's a threat to my Ren.

A man groans from the floor and stands on wobbly feet. When he regains focus, he roars at my father and pistol whips him. Everything blurs in front of me as the tears become too plentiful. We will all die here. All three of us. Two of the people I love most in the world sit in those chairs, bloody and weak. Camilo is going to end them all because of me.

I squirm against the man holding me and when his hand slips off my mouth, I manage to cry out, "Oscar! Help us!"

He charges into the container, but Camilo stops him with his harsh words. "That's enough, hijo!"

Camilo goes to stand behind Ren and grabs a handful of his hair. He yanks his head back so I can see Ren's face. His eyes slowly blink open. When they fixate on me, he utters something unintelligible before attempting to smile at me. It breaks my heart into a thousand pieces.

"Say goodbye to your lawn boy," Camilo hisses. His blade

comes into view and it takes me a half a second to realize what he's about to do. He's about to deliver the same fate to Ren that Heath did to Duvan. I should close my eyes. Not witness another horrifying act, but I refuse to abandon Ren in his last moments.

The storm must be picking up because I swear I hear chaos ensuing outside of the metal containers. I wish the storm would pick us all up and carry us out to the sea. Drowning would be quick and painless. I wouldn't have to watch those I love bleed out.

"B-Brie." Ren's reverent way of saying my name has me sobbing so hard, I can't breathe. I lock eyes with his half-lidded ones and convey every ounce of love I have for him with just one look.

Camilo's movement is quick as he slashes his knife across the front of Ren's throat. I'm frozen even as a million things happen at once. Daddy freeing a hand and throwing a punch that lands in Camilo's stomach, which jolts him. The man holding my mouth releases me as he's tackled by Oscar.

And then I'm running.

Running. Running. Running.

I have to get to him.

Movement and shadows race around me but I ignore them as I all but tackle Ren in the chair. Blood runs from a slice in his throat and it's Duvan all over again as I desperately hold my palm over the wound. I sob and kiss his bloody face.

"D-Don't leave me," I beg through my tears. "Please don't you dare leave me. I love you!"

I slide out of his lap and hit the floor. I'm on a mission to free him from this chair. Shouts and thumping of metal resound behind me, but I don't care. All that matters is untying

Ren and getting him to a hospital.

He. Will. Live.

I will not go through this. Not again.

Daddy's voice shouts at me through my haze, but I attempt to ignore it. That is until he jerks me to my feet. I scream and fight him.

"Shhhh, cariño," Diego says and flashes me a bright smile in the darkness. "I must deal with Camilo and I can't do that if you're screaming."

I'm still gaping in shock at his surprise appearance when he quickly sheds his jacket and then rips at his dress shirt. The buttons go flying everywhere and echo in the container. A quick sweep of the room shows Oscar in one of Diego's men's grip and the other of Camilo's men sprawled out on the floor. Daddy attempts to hold me back from the knife fight that is about to go down. Camilo appears enraged as he glares at Diego, his own knife out in front of him.

"Long time, viejo," Diego says as he tosses his knife back and forth between his hands.

"I spared your life last time because you were a boy," Camilo hisses. "I won't make that mistake this time."

Diego laughs, a laugh that at one time scared me. But this time, I'm thankful for it. "I bear those scars all over my face and abdomen. Scars you decorated me with. A man doesn't wear such scars without making a promise to himself to return them to the man who originally gave them to him." Lightning quick, he slashes Camilo across the belly. It's shallow but Camilo grunts in pain.

"Why are you here?" Camilo hisses as he attempts to stab at Diego. Diego is fast, though, and he gashes Camilo's forearm. The old man howls and stumbles back.

"A deal is a deal," Diego remarks and then flashes me another one of his flirty grins. "I promised the girl protection. So protection is what she shall get."

Camilo's screams of rage echo through the container. "The bitch got you too?!"

Diego does a series of quick arm movements that I soon realize are brutal stabs to Camilo's stomach. Camilo grunts and falls to his knees.

"Am I to make him suffer or am I to make him die, cariño?" Diego questions as he tosses his bloody knife back and forth between his hands again. Camilo has dropped his own knife with a clatter as he desperately attempts to block the holes in his abdomen that are gushing with blood.

Oscar fights against the man holding him. His eyes are on his father, heartbreak shining in them. If I didn't hate Camilo so much, I'd feel bad for him. Oscar jerks his gaze to me and pleads with his eyes, since his mouth is covered by his assailant.

"Make him die," I spit out, my entire body trembling with anger.

Oscar's eyes harden at my words and then he hangs his head, surely to avoid watching what's about to happen. I, however, drag my gaze over to Diego who grins at me like he's just won the biggest prize at a carnival game. I give him a nod. He lets out a hiss as he delivers a series of fatal stabs to Camilo's heart. When the old man falls forward with a *thunk*, Diego starts toward me.

Daddy growls. "Stay the fuck away from my daughter."

Diego narrows his eyes at him. "Want me to kill him too, cariño?"

I shake my head. "H-He's under my protection. As is

Oscar and..." I trail off as a sob escapes me. Ren remains unmoving in his chair. "We need to get him to a hospital. Help me," I plead.

Diego motions at one of his men. "Leave the Rojas boy. Gather this other one and put him in a vehicle." He snatches me out of my dad's grip and hauls me to him for a hug. "Thank you, cariño. You've just made me a very rich man. You're untouchable, little princess. If you need anything, even a little cock every now and again, you call Daddy Diego."

"Touch her again and you'll be Daisy Diego when I cut your dick off," Daddy barks.

Diego laughs and releases me. He struts out of the container and out of my life.

Two men pull Ren from the chair and work together to carry him from the container. Another man hits Oscar in the head with the butt of his gun. Ozzy crumples to the floor beside his father's corpse. I know he'll get out of here. Alive. And that's all that matters. But right now, I can't worry about Oscar's well-being. The most important person is Ren.

*Please God, don't let him die. I can't do this again.*

"Sweetheart, you should eat something," Baylee says, concern lacing her voice. "You're pale."

I wave away the package of crackers she attempts to hand me and swallow down the urge to puke. When I lift my gaze, her eyes are bloodshot from crying. Her bottom lip trembles.

"I love him," I admit to her. "I always have. It's just different but it's love."

She pulls me into her arms, and I break down into gut-wrenching sobs for the tenth time today. Baylee strokes my hair in a way that reminds me of how Mom would when I was upset or sick. This only saddens me more. I desperately hug her, afraid she'll suddenly leave me too.

I'm the worst kind of luck.

People who love me end up hurt. Or worse.

"Brie baby," Daddy murmurs from the chair on the other side of me. "I should take you home. You need rest."

Baylee hisses at him over my head. "Go check on my grandbaby. I can stay with her. You know it's never a good idea for Hannah to be alone."

He grunts but there is resignation in his voice. I feel him kiss the top of my head. "Call me when you hear something."

Once he's gone, I pull away from her embrace to look at her. "It's been hours. This is bad, right?"

Baylee darts her gaze to someone behind me. Then, I hear War's voice. "The probability of him living is high. If they're still in surgery, hopefully that means they've been able to repair the damage. Worse news would have been if they came out right away. At least we know they're doing something back there."

"But his throat," I murmur. "I watched Camilo slash it."

Baylee shudders and lets out a choked sob but it's War who speaks again. "Gabe described the wound to me. It doesn't sound as if it was as deep as you are thinking. You said yourself, he cut across the front. Had it been situated to one side, his carotid could have been severed but it doesn't sound like it was."

Carotid.

The same artery that was cut on my mother.

I shiver and swipe away my tears so I can look at him. Right now, with worry etched on his face, he looks so much like Ren that it makes me start crying again. He sits down beside me and pulls me against his side.

"He's going to be okay," he promises. I don't know how he can promise such things but he says it with such conviction that I believe him.

"This is all my fault," I tell him through my tears. "If I'd have just come here and abandoned Duvan's whole life, I could have avoided all this. I'm so sorry."

Baylee pats my knee. "This is not your fault, sweetheart. You were dragged into that life. And we're the ones sorry for that. Hannah started this course. She's sick and unstable. We failed her but we won't fail you and Ren."

*You and Ren.*

As if we're a team and they're our support network.

I don't know why this fills me with such joy, but it docs.

Mason stirs in his baby seat and Baylee absently rocks him. "We're here for you, Brie," she assures me and squeezes my hand. "The world has played some pretty cruel jokes on me by sending your father back into my life, only for him to fall in love with my mentally unstable child, but the joke was on me. I was given Toto." She smiles at me. "And I was given you. We're here for you."

Mom is gone. Duvan is gone. Ren is barely hanging on by a thread. But these two people are here. They provide the strength that two parents who love their children with every-thing they have. Ren is lucky to have them as parents.

"McPherson family?" a deep voice calls out.

All three of us jolt and War stalks over to the doctor. They speak in hushed tones, which makes my anxiety spike. But when War turns around to beam at me and give me a thumbs up, I break down in hysterical sobs.

He's okay.

He's going to be okay.

# PART THREE:

"We're In This Together"
by Nine Inch Nails

# XIX | Ren

AN ANNOYING BEEPING WAKES ME FROM MY SLUMBER, AND I suppress a groan. My dreams were filled with brown eyes and sweet smiles. I dreamed of Brie. A heaviness seems to hold me to my bed. I attempt to blink my eyes open to figure out what's come over me. The beeping gets more annoying but then something warm grips my hand.

"Shhhh," the sweet voice murmurs. "I'm here. Calm down."

I relax because I like the sound of her voice. Like an angel. Am I in heaven?

"My baby boy," another female voice utters.

My eyelids feel as though they have heavy lead weights attached to them, but I slowly manage to blink them open. The room is bright white and I squint against it. I hear some shuffling and the room dims. I'm able to open my eyes a little more. Dad stands at the end of my bed with Mom on his left. The angel with the pretty brown eyes sits to my left, clutching my hand.

I try to tell her she's beautiful, but my mouth doesn't seem to work. So I settle for squeezing her hand. Tears streak down her cheeks and she leans forward bringing her beautiful face near mine.

"You made it," she assures me with a tearful grin. "You didn't die on me."

I try to smile but it's too difficult.

"You're still intubated," Dad explains. "Try not to move or talk. Give it some time."

My eyes never stray from hers, though. I could stare at her for eternity.

"We're going to go grab some coffee," Mom tells the angel. "We'll give you two some time alone." Mom kisses my forehead while Dad pats my foot. Once they're gone, the beautiful one grins.

"You scared me to death," she murmurs.

Brie.

Her name is Brie.

I could never forget such a pretty name.

Sweet Gabriella. An angel in more ways than one.

"And I thought I wouldn't ever be able to tell you the words I so desperately need you to hear," she chokes out. Her lips press kisses all over my face. I close my eyes because I want to relish in the way it feels.

"I love you." She pulls away to stare down at me. "Did you hear that? I love you, Ren McPherson. I have pretty much since the first moment you looked up at me in that window. Something snapped into place then. A missing piece. A part of my heart that wasn't fully formed. You slotted yourself right in and, truth be told, never left. My heart was dragged through the mud, stomped on, shredded, and abused. And yet, at the end of it, you were still there. Still hanging on for dear life. Embedded deep inside. There wasn't much left of my heart at the end, but what was left was the part you still held on to. Here I was worried I wouldn't have room for you in my tiny sliver of a heart," she murmurs, tears freely falling down her face. "And yet the only room left was for you." She draws my hand to her chest and presses it against her, so I can feel the thundering just beneath her flesh. "My heart is yours, Ren."

I reach for her with my other hand, despite the sharp pains that pull across my torso. With shaky movements, I swipe away her tears. Then, I tug her hand to my chest, mimicking her action. My heart pounds just as hard for her. I can't say the words, but I hope she feels them. They're thick as they cloud the air around us.

*I love you too.*

With every part of my being and then some.

*You're mine, Gabriella Rojas, and I am yours.*

Fatigue threatens to steal me from Brie. I desperately attempt to burn her face into my mind, so that when I'm sleeping, I'll think only of her.

"I love you," she reminds me as my eyes blink closed.

*I love you too.*

"She had the baby," Brie tells me as she folds a small onesie and tucks it into a drawer.

"Hannah?" I question as I sit up in the rocker that's in the nursery. Pain ripples through my entire body, but I try not to let Brie know I'm hurting. She'll try and shove more pain pills down my throat. It's been three weeks since I left the hospital, but she still treats me as if I've just left surgery.

"Daddy called," she says. "It's a boy. They're calling him Land."

"After my grandpa?" I'm mildly irritated that Hannah has successfully stolen all of our grandparent's names for her babies. She always was selfish. One day I'd hoped to pass on one of their names to one of my own children.

"He wants us to come see the baby, but I told him you weren't up to it," she says softly, her back to me.

"We can go if you wan—"

She cuts me off with a wave of a hand. "I'll see him when Daddy brings him by one day. I'd rather not spend one second with your sister."

The feeling is mutual.

"How are Duvan and Alejandra today?" I question.

She turns and beams at me. Then, she rubs her stomach before dropping to the floor in front of me. Her head rests on my uninjured thigh. I stroke her hair as she lets out a contented sigh. "They're good. I think I'm finally getting cravings."

I chuckle but it makes my abdomen ache. Despite the many stab wounds Camilo inflicted, most were superficial. The one that tore a hole in my spleen was the worrisome one, which took hours to repair. Thankfully, the surgeons were excellent ones. "What sort of cravings?"

She groans and looks up at me, embarrassment tinting her cheeks. "Gross things. Like crab from that seaside restaurant I met up with Diego at." I grit my teeth but swallow back a growl. Despite my hating that prick, in the end, he did save our lives. If he protects my woman and our babies, I'll tolerate him.

"Crab is good," I say with a smile.

She shrugs. "And tacos but with ranch dressing instead of sour cream."

At this, I shake my head. "Okay, that is gross. Anything else?"

"Cherry pie filling. Like the kind out of the can." She makes a grumble of annoyance. "It sounds so good right now. Who eats that stuff straight out of the can? It's all I can think about."

I run my fingers through her silky hair and wink. "Help me out of this chair and I'll go with you right now. We'll buy twenty cans if that makes you happy."

She stands and shakes her head. "I don't think so, buddy. You're not fit to grocery shop. I'll call Calder. He'll go with me."

"And leave me here all alone with Luciana? Why do you insist upon her babysitting me, anyway? Our conversations are always one-sided." When she scoffs, I continue. "Because all she does is drone on and on about how much Calder looks like "The Beebs." I throw up in my mouth at least ten times during every conversation we have." And it's true. Luciana's fingers fly across her phone as she writes out twenty different ways to tell me how hot she thinks my brother is.

Brie laughs and clutches my hands. I wince but we finally get me to my feet. I take her cheeks, which have finally started to round out now that she's able to keep food down, and grin at her.

"When did the doctor say I could have sex again?" I tease and steal a kiss.

She rolls her eyes. "Six weeks. You're not even close,

buddy. No funny business."

I draw her closer to me, careful not to press her against my sore flesh. My cock, though, has a different plan and pokes at her belly. "You're going to deny an injured man?"

Her palm rubs against my erection and she looks up at me with a salacious stare. "I said we weren't going to have sex." Then she smirks and it's devious and goddamned beautiful. "I never said anything about blow jobs."

Before I can process her words, she's on her knees and gently tugging down my shorts and boxers.

"Did I ever tell you how much I love y—" My words die in my throat the moment her mouth wraps around my neglected cock. "Jesus Christ, woman, you're so fucking good at that." I grip her hair as she takes me deep, careful not to gag.

The woman pulls out every trick in the book until I'm murmuring her beautiful name over and over again in a chant.

She sucks me dry, and I hiss in pain the moment my stomach clenches with my release. The moment she pops off my cock and looks up at me with my seed running down her chin and a happy smile on her face, I know right then…

No matter what storms come our way, we'll endure them. Together.

Because our love is strong and unflappable.

Love destroys demons and obliterates broken pasts.

Love is ours—finally—and we fucking earned it.

# XX | Brie

*Two months later...*

HIS MOUTH IS ON MY SWOLLEN TIT AND HE'S DRIVING ME crazy by sucking on the flesh everywhere except my needy nipple. My state of duress has the babies rolling around like wild in my stomach.

"Staaaahp," I complain in the darkness.

He pulls away and soon the light from the lamp floods the room. His dark brows are pulled together in concern. "Is everything okay? Are my little cubs okay in there?" His large hands splay over my big round belly. The babies respond to his touch and roll around some more. A look of pure joy passes over his features.

"They're fine," I assure him with a smile.

My hands cover his and I stare at him as he watches my stomach.

"I still can't get over how weird this feels. To touch them. I mean, I felt Mason in my mom's stomach, but this is different.

They're…" he trails off as if he doesn't want to say anything to hurt me.

"They're yours?" I finish.

His steely blue eyes dart to mine, and the heat in them nearly scorches me. "Ours."

I nod and clutch his hand. He starts talking to the babies, but I'm distracted by his bare torso. Three months ago, he was toned and flawless. Since he can't work out much yet, his defined lines aren't as prominent. It's his scars that haunt me, though. One day they'll fade to silvery white but right now they're still puffy and dark pink. A daily reminder that he almost died. When I sniffle, he curls up beside me and pulls me into his strong arms.

"What's wrong, beautiful?"

I swallow down my emotion. "Nothing. I just think about how I almost lost you from time to time, and it upsets me."

He sits up on one elbow and frowns at me. My gaze falls to the red scar across his neck. That one affects me the most. That one I see whether he's dressed or not. That one reminds me that he was lucky when Mom and Duvan were not. I reach up and tenderly stroke the pink flesh.

Understanding washes over him and he gently plucks my hand away. He pins it on the bed and a low growl rumbles from him.

"I'm not going to wither away," he tells me, his gaze fierce. If I had any doubts that he isn't as strong as he once was, they get squashed under that tough look he's giving me. His grip is firm and unmovable as he holds my wrist against the bed. "Now tell me how you want to be fucked, little momma."

I laugh and spread my legs. "Just like this. So I can see you."

His brow arches as he makes a point to stare at my big belly. "And how exactly do you think we'll manage?"

Sticking out my tongue, I grab my pillow and swat it at him. "Put this under my ass," I instruct in a bossy tone. "Then fuck me from your knees where I can watch."

An evil smirk quirks up his features. "My bossy girl is so dirty. I love it." He folds the pillow in half and slips it beneath me. Then, he slides a leg over each of his broad shoulders. His cock is thick and heavy as it rests against my bare pussy. From this vantage point, I can see all of his scars. It sickens me yet it reminds me that he's made it through alive.

"Fuck me, Daddy," I tease.

He laughs and gives my clit a tiny pinch that has me shuddering with need. "You're a bad girl."

I bite on my bottom lip and that steals his smile. Pure, starved need paints his handsome features as he grabs my hips and then slides into my very wet opening. I let out a ragged sound of bliss as he bucks into me slowly.

"Camilo said I had a magical cunt. Does it feel different to you?" I question, suddenly overwhelmed with need to know what makes me so special.

Ren rolls his eyes at me. "Are you seriously wanting to discuss this with my cock nine inches deep inside you?"

I let out a gasp when he gives my clit a little slap. It sends ripples of pleasure surging through me. "Just tell me."

He shakes his head as he thrusts into me hard. "It's not your pussy that makes you so special. I mean"—he flashes me a wolfish grin—"I love it. Don't get me wrong. But to me, it's your…"

His cock slides out of me and then he rolls me over onto my side. "On your knees, beautiful," he barks out. I get on my elbows and knees and wriggle my ass at him. He enters me hard enough to make me cry out. Then he slaps my ass.

"Oh, God," I moan and push back against him, meeting him thrust for thrust.

"Baby, this ass is what grown men turn fucking stupid over. It's perfect." Thrust. Slap. Another moan from me. "And it's mine."

"I'll be back in a bit," he murmurs, kissing my cheek before turning out the light. "Rest and then I'll feed you and those babies some ranch tacos."

I'm smiling even as I hear the front door slam shut and his truck drive away. Ren is the only man I know that doesn't even seem bothered to have to go hunt his woman some tacos down at midnight. My tummy grumbles. God, I really do love him.

After our wild fuck session, I'm tired despite my hunger. I find myself drifting in and out. When I hear the bedroom door creak open, I smile. Rolling over, I seek out my man.

"Were you able to get any?" I question.

But when he emerges from the shadows, and a sliver of moonlight from the window reveals his face, I'm frozen. A million emotions filter through me all at once.

"Looking stunning all naked, mi amor," he murmurs.

I blink in confusion. This is real. This isn't a dream.

"W-What are you doing here?" I stammer.

A low growl rumbles from him as he takes another step toward the bed. In an effort to hide, I drag the sheet up my naked flesh.

"Are you pregnant with my child?"

Emotion clogs my throat and no words come out. I don't understand.

"Duvan?"

# XXI
## Brie

"Oh, sourpuss," he utters softly. "Don't I wish I could give my brother back to you, but he's gone. Oscar gave me an urn with his ashes. Duvan is dead."

Bile rises in my throat as I fretfully look around for a weapon, shaking off the vision of my dead husband. Esteban isn't the cocky manipulator he once was. In fact, he appears ragged and not at all put together. His hair is messy and he's sporting some scruff. It's as though he's been hiding under some rock until now. "You need to leave, Esteban." No longer do I get a surge of need whenever I see him. Terror and helplessness and despair are what consume me. My hand clutches my belly in a subconscious desire to protect my children.

He stalks forward and then pounces. Like the black panther I always equated him to. This tigress isn't and never was a worthy adversary. I cry out as he pushes my wrists together and pins them above my head. His heavy body straddles my waist. A sob escapes me when he runs his large palm over my breast to my stomach. The babies roll in response.

His lips curl into a proud grin but I don't miss the possessive gleam in his eyes. "Is. This. Baby. Mine?" Then, his voice drops as he reaches for my face. "We fucked countless times, sourpuss." As if I need the reminder.

I spit at him. "Fuck you! Get out of my house!"

His brows crash together as hurt flashes in his eyes. "Is this baby mine?" he demands, irritation lacing his tone. "Your stomach is so big. You're further along, which means it's mine."

"Babies. They're your brother's *babies*. The doctor confirmed when I conceived."

Dark eyes widen in surprise. Then, a fleeting look of anger. "I've come for you."

I'm already shaking my head. "I'm not going anywhere with you! Leave, Esteban!"

He growls before reaching back and slapping my face. Not hard, but enough to have me dazed. "She's so lonely. I'm bringing you so she has someone to entertain her."

Her?

"I don't know what you're talking about," I argue, my voice becoming weaker by the second. But I do. Deep down, I do. And it sickens me.

"That would hurt little Red's feelings," he chides. "It's a shame how easily she was forgotten by her best friend."

Ice runs cold through my veins. I gave up months ago assuming one of Camilo or Diego's men or even Esteban had killed Vee.

"Y-You have Vee?" I stammer out in surprise.

His smile is tender and it confuses me. "I do. She is

mine now."

I buck underneath him, but he's too strong. "Let me go! Tell me where she is, you fucking asshole!" I rage at him.

"I'll do better. I'll take you to her, sourpuss," he assures me with a cold grin.

I hear a sound behind him and then see the gleam of the baseball bat I keep behind the bedroom door.

"The hell you will," Ren roars a second before I hear the crack of the bat.

Esteban howls and rolls away from me. Ren pounces without hesitation, swinging that bat like he's trying to nail a homerun right out of the park. The cracking of Esteban's ribs is loud, and it makes me gag.

"Ren! Stop!" I screech and scramble to put myself between him and Esteban. But I'm too late. Ren swings another hard blow that hits Esteban right in the back of the head. The sickening pop actually does make me ill. I burst off the bed and rush into the bathroom, barely making it to the toilet in time to expel my guts. The bat clatters to the tile floor as Ren drops behind me, his hands flitting all over me checking for injuries.

"Is he dead?" I question through my tears.

He shakes his head. "I don't think so."

"Good!" I shriek. When he glowers at me, I quickly continue. "He knows where Vee is!"

Understanding washes over him. And then relief. "Call 911."

As soon as the call is made and help is on the way, I make my way back into the bedroom. Seeing Esteban bloody and helpless and unconscious causes my chest to tighten. It feels right. Like he deserves it and so much more. Full

231

fucking circle. Not long ago, it was him staring over me, wielding all the power. I was his victim.

Not anymore.

## Three days later...

"Sit down, woman," Ren orders and points his paintbrush at me.

I pout but do as I'm told. He looks hot as ever in a pair of holey jeans that hang low on his hips, revealing just a tiny view of his ass crack. Since he's painting, he's not wearing a shirt, and his entire tattooed back is on display for my visual pleasure. The entire thing is covered in his intricate tree. His tiger and cubs have long been filled in. It's beautiful and I love it.

With a smile, I rub my belly. "Are you sure you can paint those stripes? I think this looks harder than the YouTube video tutorial."

He looks over his shoulder and gives me a smoldering look. "Keep mouthing off and I'll have to keep that pretty mouth busy so I can paint in peace."

Laughing, I shoot him the bird. "Real funny."

We're quiet again as he paints. Ren truly is beautiful both inside and out. Sometimes I worry I don't tell him that enough.

"I love you," I blurt out.

He gives me a lopsided grin over his shoulder that has my

heart thumping in my chest. "I love you too."

When he goes back to painting, I have the urge to say more. "I know I don't tell you enough but you mean the world to me. You were always there for me. Nobody has been there every step of the way like you have." My chin wobbles.

He sets his brush down and struts over to me. I find myself ogling this sexy-ass man who I can proudly call mine. His fingers grip my jaw, and he tilts my head up so he can kiss me. It's brief and sweet, but it knocks me over with his love. With Ren, I feel it rippling from him at all times. With Ren, I never feel his love waver.

"Thank you," I murmur against his warm lips.

He pulls away and something like pride shines in his eyes as he regards me. "Loving you is easy, Bric. Nothing about it ever feels like a chore. It's a gift. So thank you for my gift." He winks at me before making his way over to his project.

My mind is on thoughts of our future. One where Ren is my husband and these kids call him Daddy. Thoughts of us going to T-ball games together, dinners and holidays with his wonderful family, late nights where he and I worship each other's bodies, family pictures and school plays. Normalcy. The American dream.

Love.

Ours.

My phone starts to ring and I see it's Daddy calling. He probably wants to drop by and visit. I refuse to admit it to anyone but I'm in love with my new little brother. It gives me a sneak peek of what it will be like to have my own babies. Sometimes, I hold baby Land for hours and inhale his sweet scent. Daddy is smart enough to leave the psycho with her parents when he brings my siblings by.

"Hey," I answer as my eyes drag back over to Ren. He's been able to work out a little more here and there. Painting will probably leave him tired, but he's insistent. I admire his back muscles while Daddy hisses on the other line. It takes me a second to pull my attention back to my phone call. "Wait? What? Say that again," I demand.

"Esteban escaped from the hospital," he snarls. "Tell Ren to put a bullet through anyone's skull who tries to come into your house."

Ren, sensing my distress, is already stalking over to me, wearing an alarmed expression.

"But he hasn't told them where Vee is yet," I mutter. "He can't escape. We have to find her."

Daddy grumbles on the line. "I'm sorry about your friend, but that's the least of my worries right now. My worry is your safety. I'll be over in fifteen minutes. Call your fuck-face *friend*, who still has a death sentence."

When he hangs up, I stare up at Ren.

"What is it?" he demands and falls to his knees in front of me. He takes my hand and kisses the top of it. Fierce love and protectiveness shine in his gaze.

"Esteban escaped." I blink in shock. Then, I dial my "fuck-face friend who still has a death sentence." I will *not* let my dreams and future with Ren be compromised by a madman.

"Ahhh, cariño. Ready for the big D?" his deep voice purrs as he answers.

I swallow and choke out my words. "It..It's Esteban. He escaped."

His breath rushes out in a hiss. "Ever since he got to you a few days ago, I've had men parked on your street watching. He won't get to you," he assures me.

"I'm not worried about me." And I'm not. At least not one hundred percent. This is bigger. "We have to find him. When we find him, we find her."

Diego chuckles on the other end. "Are you asking me for a favor, cariño?"

"Por favor."

# EPILOGUE
## Vee

**H**E LEFT ME.

Promised to bring me something that would make me happy. What a ridiculous concept. *Happy.* I don't even understand what that means anymore. How can one be happy in a metal box with no light, no entertainment, no one to talk to? Nothing.

My stomach growls and the pains are too much to bear. I've slowly been starving to death. At first, I picked through the rations and attempted to share them with my mother. But she was too far gone on the heroin to care. She screamed and clawed, and at one point, tried to attack me as if I held her precious drug prisoner.

Newsflash, we were the prisoners.

But then the strangest thing happened. She stopped screaming and hissing and fighting. She stopped breathing altogether. And the moment it all became quiet, I let out a sigh of relief. My mother died from withdrawals. From a drug she'd never touched until Esteban forced it into her vein. And

I was glad.

Not that I didn't love her.

I did.

Truly.

But she became some savage beast the moment he put us in this cage. He took joy in making her dependent on him for a simple high. But I depended on him for something altogether different.

A sob escapes me but no tears roll out. Sometimes I wish he had forced the heroin on me. Mom was blissed out of her mind for most of the months we've been here. I've been clear headed. I have been awake and coherent every time he's come for me.

I imagine his large body curled around mine. At one time it made me shudder. At one time I hated him. Hated that he stole so much from me. But now, I miss him. I miss his warmth. I miss his words in my lonely world. I miss the food he would feed me.

Why did he leave me?

I know I won't survive much longer without him. Mom's body has begun to decompose over in the corner. She didn't last a full day without the constant stream of drugs in her system. Since she didn't have medicine to help her withdrawal, she simply shut down. Her moans and screams are no more, but now I'm completely alone.

My mind begs to think about my past. Dad and Brie. Oscar. Even Ren and Calder. The funny thing is, though, I can't remember any of them. Oscar's face, because it's so similar to Esteban's, is the only one I can clutch onto through the haze.

Each and every time I attempt to remember my friends

and family, only one frighteningly handsome face comes to mind. And I miss it. I would give myself willingly to him if he would just come back and save me from this slow, painful death.

Diabla Roja.

I smile in the darkness and touch the thin mattress where he used to sleep with me sometimes. If I close my eyes, I can almost smell him. Spicy and manly. In the early days, he would take my orgasms. I'd fought him tooth and nail, but in the end, I always gave in. Gave him what he wanted—what we both wanted.

"Diabla Roja."

I start crying because now I'm delirious. I can almost hear him. Am I dying?

"Shhhhh."

It's as though his palms are whispering touches along my outer arm. As if his fingers are running through my ratty red hair.

"You're alive." His phantom voice sounds real. Pained and desperate and relieved. "Can you stand, Roja?"

I blink slowly and roll toward the sounds that tease me. It's dark but I see his shadow looming above me. "Esteban?" I croak.

His palm strokes my cheek. "I went to fetch her for you. So you wouldn't cry so much," he tells me, his voice sad. "But then that motherfucker put me in the hospital. All I could think about was how you were starving here."

A tear slides down my temple. This is real. He came back for me. "I don't want her," I rasp out. "I need you."

He grunts as if he's in pain but he manages to scoop my weak frame from the mattress on the floor. With labored breaths, he carries me right past my mother's rancid body and out of the metal box. It's the first time in months I've left this prison. I let out a relieved sob and cling to his shirt.

"Shhh," he murmurs as he carries me through the darkness. Gently, he loads me into the car. As he drives, I simply stare at him. Such a simple gift, the gift of sight, I'm able to use on him. Drinking in his every feature. His longish black hair normally remains slicked back but today hangs in his eyes. Those calculating, nearly black eyes that dart over to me every so often. The scruff on his cheeks that my fingers crave to touch. We drive for what seems like forever until he pulls up to a secluded house on the beach.

"Where are we?" I'm shivering despite his hand constantly rubbing on my thigh in an oddly comforting manner.

"One of my father's safe houses. I sometimes stay here when I need to keep a low profile," he tells me before climbing out of the car. I don't have the energy to move. When he opens my car door, I drag my gaze to look at him in the moonlight. He reminds me of a hungry wolf. Starved for me.

Well, I'm starved too.

"I'm hungry," I tell him.

He nods and scoops me up. "I know, Roja. I'm going to fix you right up."

My heart thunders at his words. I believe them. I want him to fix me.

I'm in a daze for the next few hours. He feeds me broth and holds me. Eventually, he gets me under the hot spray of the shower. After not having properly bathed in months, it feels like heaven. I bawl until the water runs cold and I'm hiccupping and he has to carry my shivering body out. When he sets me on the bed, panic races up my spine. I clutch onto the front of his shirt and whine.

"Don't leave me."

His brows furrow and he strokes my wet hair. "Never again."

I wake for the first time in what feels like forever, comfortable and warm. A big hot body is draped over me. I'm not sure if he's trying to keep me from running or to keep me warm. I burrow further beneath him to seek out his protection. My movement wakes him as well.

"Let me see you," he murmurs, his voice gruff with sleep.

I tilt my head up and stare into his nearly black eyes. At one time, they terrified me. Months ago, when he'd take what he wanted whenever he wanted, I feared him with every fiber of my being. I prayed for someone to come save me.

Nobody came.

And then the strangest thing happened. I became reliant on him. He was the only person who wanted me. Everyone else forgot about me. So, soon, despite my outward denial, I came to look forward to his late night visits. I would bask in his expert touches and come from his fingers on my own accord. I'd never admitted I wanted him until now.

"I was so lonely," I choke out, my eyes welling with hot tears. "I thought I was going to die."

He lets out a fierce growl before his mouth finds mine. In the past, whenever he'd kiss me, I never participated. I'd lain there like a dead doll. Now, I crave his mouth more than the broth I desperately downed last night. My mouth parts and I shove my tongue into his. Every nerve ending in my body fires to life. I squirm with the need for him to touch me everywhere.

"What's come over you?" he murmurs against my lips as his palm roams over my round breast. He tweaks the nipple, which makes me cry out. Then, his hand trails down south toward my pussy.

"I…I…I just need…"

His finger grazes my clit and I jolt with a moan. A growl of approval resounds from him and it seems to stroke my poor, fragile heart. I want him to be happy with me. I want to be enough.

"Open your legs, Roja. Let me see you," he murmurs, his lips trailing down to my throat.

Like a whore, I jerk my knees apart to give him what he wants. His finger dips inside me dragging a mewl from me. "Oh, please…I need more."

He nips at my neck just as he inches another finger inside me. Before Esteban, I was a virgin. That first time had been painful, but every other time was surprisingly pleasure filled.

"Always so wet for me, Roja," he praises, his fingers working magic on my insides. "I see you've finally come to learn who owns this perfect cunt."

I nod and bite my lip. His mouth kisses along my chest until he has my pebbled nipple between his teeth. I grab my knee and pull it toward me. His two fingers aren't enough. I crave him. Deeper. Harder. His cock stretching me wide.

"What do you want?" he questions as his thumb begins working lazy circles on my clit while he fucks me with two fingers.

"I need you," I moan. "Please."

His fingers slip out of me, and I yelp at the loss. I'm squirming and helpless as he grabs a condom from the end table. It takes all of ten seconds to sheath his cock, but it's ten seconds too long. Thankfully, he climbs on top of me and suffocates me with his addicting presence. Our eyes lock when the tip of his cock teases my opening in a delightful way.

"You want this?" he demands, his free hand delicately stroking my throat.

I grab his wrist and nod.

With a powerful thrust, he drives into me. Hard. I scream in pleasure as I desperately claw his shoulders. He winces in pain but then quickly finds his stride. Esteban drives into me as if this single act will mold my soul to his.

I close my eyes and give myself to him.

The dead heart in my chest belongs to this man. It may not beat, but it's his.

"You belong to me, Roja," he growls, his grip on my throat tightening.

I let out a hissed "yessss" as my body ripples with desire. His mouth hovers over mine as he fucks me senseless. I become an animal the moment my orgasm explodes through me and I claw his flesh, needing to crawl inside him. His grunts and then the swelling of his cock tells me he finds his release too.

Esteban relaxes on me and nuzzles his nose against my ear. It's perfection, and I don't want to leave this moment. But then the phone on the bedside table is ringing and he's leaving me to answer it. I lick my lips as I watch him pull the wet condom off his large cock. He smirks as he answers. The voice on the other line is familiar. It jolts me out of my sex-induced fog and sends a shiver of memories down my spine. I can't make out all the words but I do hear some.

*Thump.*

*Thump.*

Why does my chest hurt?

"This is war, brother. We're going to slaughter every single one of Diego's men. Then…" The line goes quiet for a moment. "Then we take back our empire."

*Thump.*

Oscar.

*Thump.*

My simple world consisting of me and Esteban fucking all day suddenly dissipates as clarity sets in.

*Thump.*

I'm going to see Oscar.

*Thump.*

The dead heart in my chest thuds back to life.

*Thump.*

Because it's only ever truly beat for one man.

Coming Soon!
The saga continues in…
## This Isn't Fair, Baby

# PLAYLIST

Listen on Spotify

"Mess Is Mine" by Vance Joy

"Strange Magic" by Electric Light Orchestra

"Are You Alone Now?" By Dead Sea Empire

"Closer" by Nine Inch Nails

"Don't You (Forget About Me)" by Simple Minds

"Love is Strange" by Mickey & Sylvia

"Bloodstream" by Stateless

"Monster" by Meg Myers

"I Will Possess Your Heart" by Death Cab for Cutie

"Love the Way You Lie" by Eminem

"We're In This Together" by Nine Inch Nails

"To Be Alone" by Hozier

"Heart Heart Head" by Meg Myers

"Even Though Our Love Is Doomed" by Garbage

"Sorry" by Meg Myers

"Ain't No Sunshine When She's Gone" by Black Label Society

"#1 Crush" by Garbage

"Unsteady" by X Ambassadors

"Not an Addict" by K's Choice

"Can't Help Falling In Love" by Elvis Presley

"You Caught My Eye" by Big Wreck

"Someone Like You" by Adele

"Fade Into You" by Mazzy Star

"Love Is Not Enough" by Nine Inch Nails

"Don't Walk Away" by The Mayfield Four

"Stay With Me" by Sam Smith

"The Way" by Saigon Kick

"Last Goodbye" by Jeff Buckley

"I Will Wait" by Mumford & Sons

"Team" by Lorde

"No One's Gonna Love You" by Band of Horses

"Breathe Me" by Sia

"Black" by Pearl Jam

"In Your Eyes" by Peter Gabriel

"My Songs Know What You Did In The Dark" by Fall Out
Boys

# ACKNOWLEDGEMENTS

Thank you to my husband. Matt, you're supportive and loving and more than I could ever ask for in a husband. I love you to the moon and back.

I want to thank the people who read this beta book early and gave me incredible support. Jessica Hollyfield, Elizabeth Clinton, Ella Stewart, Amanda Soderlund, Amy Bosica, Shannon Martin, Brooklyn Miller, Robin Martin, Amy Simms, Sunny Borek, and Jessica Viteri. (I hope I didn't forget anyone.) You guys always provide AMAZING feedback. You all give me helpful ideas to make my stories better and give me incredible encouragement. I appreciate all of your comments and suggestions. Love you ladies!

Also, a big thank you to Vanessa Renee Place for proofreading our story after editing. You always save me in a pinch and I can't thank you enough!! Love ya!

A huge thank you to Bex Lovesbooks for not only proofing my story but making me the MOST WONDERFUL book trailer ever!! I died over and over again watching that. You're amazing!

A big thank you to my author friends who have given me your friendship and your support. You have no idea how much that means to me.

Thank you to all of my blogger friends both big and small that go above and beyond to always share my stuff. You all rock! #AllBlogsMatter

I'm especially thankful for my Krazy for K Webster's Books reader group. You ladies are wonderful with your support and friendship. Each and every single one of you is amazingly supportive and caring. #Cucumbers4Life

I am totally thankful for my author group, the COPA gals, for being there when I need to take a load off and whine. Y'all rock!

Vanessa Bridges and Jessica D. from Prema Editing, thanks so much for editing our book! You ladies rock!

Thank you Stacey Blake for being a super star as always when formatting my books and in general. I love you! I love you! I love you!

A big thanks to my PR gal, Nicole Blanchard. You are fabulous at what you do and keep me on track!

Lastly but certainly not least of all, thank you to all of the wonderful readers out there that are willing to hear my story and enjoy my characters like I do. It means the world to me!

# ABOUT THE AUTHOR

K Webster is the author of dozens of romance books in many different genres including contemporary romance, historical romance, paranormal romance, dark romance, romantic suspense, and erotic romance. When not spending time with her husband of thirteen years and two adorable children, she's active on social media connecting with her readers.

Her other passions besides writing include reading and graphic design. K can always be found in front of her computer chasing her next idea and taking action. She looks forward to the day when she will see one of her titles on the big screen.

Join K Webster's newsletter to receive a couple of updates a month on new releases and exclusive content. To join, all you need to do is go here (http://authorkwebster.us10.list-manage.com/subscribfe?u=36473e274a1bf9597b508ea72&id=96366bb08e).

Facebook: www.facebook.com/authorkwebster

Blog: authorkwebster.wordpress.com/

Twitter:twitter.com/KristiWebster

Email: kristi@authorkwebster.com

Goodreads: www.goodreads.com/user/show/10439773-k-webster

Instagram: instagram.com/kristiwebster

Made in the USA
Lexington, KY
02 April 2018